Mama Said

An Angels of Darkness Anthology

Edited by J.V. Sadler and Lori Titus

Mama Said: An Angels of Darkness Anthology

Mama Said © 2026 by J.V. Sadler

E-book ISBN: 979-8-9896242-6-3

Paperback ISBN: 979-8-9896242-7-0

Library of Congress Control Number: 2026904865

Editors: J.V. Sadler and Lori Titus

Authors By Story Appearance: E.A. Noble, Lori Titus, Vivienne Neal, C.Y. Marshall, N.M. Chaney, Anniee Bee, J.V. Sadler, Ginny Davis, Miracle Austin, Tessa Lee-Thomas

Acknowledgements

Thank you to the Angels of Darkness (Black Women Horror Writers) social media group on Facebook for helping make this collection happen! And another thank you to all the crowdfund donors who contributed to fund this project. If you're a Black Woman horror writer, come join us:

Group QR Code

<u>Current Online Group Admins</u>

C.Y. Marshall (Group Founder), E.M. Lacey, Lori Titus, Dahlia DeWinters

<u>Anthology Planning Team</u>

Miracle Austin

Miracle Austin is a Texan YA/NA author. *Doll* is her debut YA supernatural, coming-of-age novel with diverse themes intertwined; it won second place in the Young Adult category in the 2016 *Purple DragonFly* Awards. She loves Marvel/DC, horror, 80s music, *Stranger Things/Wednesday*, and daydreaming up stories. Instagram: @MiracleAustin7.

E.M. Lacey

E.M. Lacey brews fiction with a dash of caffeine. She crafts dark urban, dystopian, and speculative tales filled with diverse characters. When not writing, she curates coffee memes, watches horror movies and anime, and reads books. You can find her at comic cons and nerdy gatherings, bonding with fellow enthusiasts. Website: www.emlacey.com.

C.Y. Marshall

I am an avid horror lover and writer who enjoys writing stories that evokes fear. Being the author of eight books my stories range from female serial killers to blood sucking vampires. Get lost in one of my books and familiar with the characters. They are waiting to become your friend.

J.V. Sadler

J.V. Sadler is a writer and poet from Cincinnati, Ohio. Her work has been featured on NIGHTLIGHT: A Horror Fiction Podcast. Her first book Licking is a collection of macabre horror short stories. You can find all her socials and links at linktr.ee/JVSadler.

Lori Titus

Lori Titus is a writer who loves fantastic and scary things.

Our awesome Kickstarter supporters

Bronze Tier – $70 or more

James 'The Great Old One' Burke, Daniel Abson, Luis Castillo

Silva

Silver Tier – $30 or more

Aren, Aubrey Thamann, Dino Hicks, Rob Grimoire

Gold Tier – $50 or more

Nicole Chaney, Jo Griffith, E.A. Noble, Bea Fernandes

Contents

Introduction
J. V. Sadler

Some may ask, "Where are all the Black horror writers?" Considering all that Black people across the diaspora have survived and thrived through, there would be more of us using the horror genre as a vehicle to transform our pain into art.

The truth is, we've always been here. Black horror writers and, by extension, Black genre fiction writers (sci-fi, speculative, fantasy, etc.) have ALWAYS been here. Mainstream literature may not reflect Black horror's vastness, but the indie world is filled to the brim with unique and utterly terrifying Black horror creations.

Despite the public's often performative calls for "support Black women," "support small businesses," or "BlackWritersMatter," Black indie writers and publishers are constantly pushed into the margins, out of sight, and into non-existence; many of us struggle with financial strain and overwork amongst other matters.

Black horror is here. Black horror writers are here. We've always been here and will stay no matter what. But it is loud, public, and continuing support that helps artists thrive. The very fact that you've picked up this anthology is a testament to your real support. Dear reader, Thank You.

I didn't write this introduction just to badmouth some looming, evil, capital "I" Industry. I don't want to be the cranky old man yelling at the young whippersnappers to get off his lawn. Instead, I want to talk about *Mama Said* and how this collection is a testament to the power of Black horror.

These stories come from a range of authors, whether veteran, award-winning authors or blossoming writers whose first publication is this very anthology. The planning team, consisting of J.V. Sadler (me!), Miracle Austin, E.M. Lacey, C.Y. Marshall, and Lori Titus, has been working on this since around May 2024. I posted my idea to organize an anthology in the Angels of Darkness Facebook group, and these awesome women really stepped up to the plate. This was my first time creating an anthology like this. Y'all, indie anthologies are hard! Kudos to those independent publishers and creators who do this work on the regular. To have a final product after overcoming so many obstacles is a relief. It was definitely a learning curve. I will take with me a lot of lessons for the next time I want to be involved in something like this.

The theme for the *Mama Said* anthology is Dark Fantasy. We collected submissions from Black women writers, giving examples of *Pan's Labyrinth* or any Tim Burton work. We initially asked for PG-13 material with no explicit or graphic materials, but I think some of the stories *really* push that boundary. So parents, please review.

Next, we were very clear that we would NOT accept any A.I .-generated stories. In anthologies, there may be times when we have our favorite stories and our least favorites; sometimes, we love them all collectively. *Mama Said* intentionally includes a range of stories, from a range of authors, with a range of writing experiences. I say this, *Mama Said* does something very important: reclaims the human element in art. It wasn't necessarily about choosing the cream of the crop of fantastical horror stories. It was about giving Black indie authors the chance to develop themselves and expose their art to the world. We develop our craft through doing. We become writers through writing. That is enough.

The stories range from bloody murder to an HBCU student's road trip gone terribly wrong. In keeping with the theme, each story captures something horrific in the fantastical . . . or something fantastic in the horrifying. We begin the anthology with "To Double Dutch the Devil," a cautionary tale with a new approach on the phrase "Be careful what you wish for." The last story, "The Whispering Well," tells of a plagued community where its fictionalized elements mirror the real-life fears and struggles of activists and community organizers.

As I close out this introduction (don't worry, you'll hear from me again in the Afterword), I want to speak directly to the spirit of *Mama Said: An Angels of Darkness Anthology*. I love you, *Mama Said*. Through the good times and the bad times, the excitement and the delays . . . you have transformed so many lives through your existence. My first time as an editor. The Black women writers who get to celebrate their first publication. The veterans who can add another publication to their belt. *Mama Said*, you are small but mighty. Very mighty! Prosper, *Mama Said*. I hope that in the years to come, someone will discover you and in them a fire of creativity will ignite. I hope that in the first month or so of your official publication, you find the attention, support, and love that you deserve. I say again, I love you, *Mama Said*.

~ J.V. Sadler

2025

To Double Dutch the Devil

E.A. Noble

It was the kind of Mississippi summer that clung to my skin like honey, thick and sticky. Cicadas screamed in the trees, their shrill calls echoing through the small town of Tallahatchie. The pavement shimmered under the high noon sun, and the air smelled of dirt roads and Ford F-150s.

Out on the cracked sidewalk, beneath the shade of a gnarled oak tree, I was tangled in jump-rope. One of my besties, Evie, with two colorful high ponytails, watched on impatiently.

"Not like that, CeeCee!" Evie tapped her sneaker on the crunchy, dry grass with her hand on her hip. "It's one, two. One, two. It's not that hard."

"For you it ain't!" I untangled myself and tried again. I flipped the beaded rope up over my head, and before I could lift a heel off the ground, the rope hit the soles of my feet, and down I went.

"I can't do this!" I screamed. I was frustrated with myself more than anything. Three months, we worked hard to get our routine together, only for Evie to sprain her ankle, leaving us to scramble for a new routine. Evie became the turner and I the jumper. The Double Dutch competition was the biggest event happening in this small town. It was a chance to finally see the world, and I was holding my team back because I couldn't land the jumps.

I lay on the hot concrete staring into the beaming sun.

"My momma said, if you stare into the sun, you'll go blind," Evie said, blocking out the sun rays. The ends of her rainbow braids swept her shoulders.

My momma would bury herself on a hot Tuesday if I got any color in my hair.

"Well, it ain't happened yet." I sat up, trying not to sound bitter.

"That's yo' problem, your attitude. Whenever you feel like you aren't perfect, you get down on yourself, and pouty. That only makes you do worse."

"But it's up to me to get us the win. I got to get the tricks right. Tasha jumps worse than me, and you sprained your ankle." I pointed to her wrapped foot.

"Yeah, and I get that, but we are a team, remember? We in this together!" Evie gazed behind me, shielding her eyes like a visor.

I heard Tasha coming before I turned around and saw her. Sneakers dragging in the dirt, potato chip bag rattling in her hands.

"The candy lady was out of icebergs, but she had these popsicles." Tasha handed me the double popsicles that broke in two, then wiped her fingers on her t-shirt which jiggled her pot belly.

I turned my nose up at the popsicles that were half melted, but took them anyway.

"What candy lady runs out of icebergs in this heat?" Evie asked, ripping her popsicles open.

Tasha shrugged; her tongue dyed a muddy brown from a Kool-Aid pickle stuffed with Flamin' Hot Cheetos.

"Okay." I dusted my blue jean shorts off and grabbed the jump rope. "Now that we're all back. Let's get to work."

"Again, CeeCee? We've been practicing since morning." Tasha huffed.

"And we gon' practice some more until we get it right." I handed her the extra beaded jump rope. "How bad do y'all want to win? Don't y'all want to make it to New York? If we can't even beat the Bettys in this old dumb town, what makes you think we will win against those city girls?"

"Winning ain't everything," Evie said.

I whirled around to her. "Winning is winning. If we ain't aiming to take it all, why are we competing? Let's just quit."

Evie sucked her teeth. Tasha rolled her eyes.

"This is supposed to be fun," Evie mumbled.

"It'll be fun when we make it to New York!"

"My stomach hurts." Tasha rubbed her belly. The Kool Aid-Hot-Cheeto-pickle was down to a few bites. "I think I'm gonna go home."

"You can't!" I said.

"Me too, my ankle is acting up again. Plus, my momma just bought me the new DVD of Sailor Moon that was released last month."

"Sailor Moon more important than winning?" I shouted.

Evie, slightly limping, and Tasha, still rubbing her belly, both glanced at each other, then at me.

"Yes," they said in unanimous laughter.

"Fine! Leave!"

"And we will!" Evie threw her arm around Tasha's neck. They both walked away, down brown streets, and over grass fields of nothing.

They didn't understand how important this was. For me, for us. I didn't want to waste away in a shotgun house surrounded by backwater, egg collecting, collard green picking old folks. I wanted to see the world, the high rises, all the people, the opportunity. To be someone different. New York would open those doors for something better. I just knew it.

I loosened the jump rope from around my neck, took a deep breath, and jumped. One–two, one–two, skipping to my own tunes.

"Miss Mary Mack, Mack, Mack . . ."

A deep voice singing startled me out of concentration.

"All dressed in black, black, black . . ."

A tall man, in a dark suit, black sunglasses, and pale skin eclipsed the sun, casting me in shadow. I locked eyes with him, giving him a stank face, as I halted my jumps.

"With silver buttons, buttons, buttons . . ." The man smiled. Sharp teeth. Gums far too red. "All down her back, back, back . . ." He held out a red sucker.

"Here," he said. "Take it."

The man's skin looked like vanilla ice cream melting painstakingly slow under a lamp light. This weirdo gave me chills, and that was hard to do when it was ninety degrees out here.

"Nah, I'm good." I stepped away, searching behind him for any signs of passersby.

He undid the wrapper, gently pulling each side apart into four neat pieces. He popped the candy into his mouth. More of him liquefied under the Mississippi sun.

I clutched the rope tight, my palms rubbing against the nylon. I was about to run when I noticed I couldn't lift my leg. It was as if I was frozen. Beads of sweat slid between my brows down the ridge of my nose. My body crawled as if ants were marching along my skin.

Momma said if a perv ever corners me, scream! But I couldn't seem to lift my tongue to do so.

"You should have taken the sweet treat, Miss Celiah Marie Jackson."

"How do you know my name?" My heart sped—ticking bombs inside my chest.

"I know everyone's name. Your best friends. Evieanna James. Tasha La'quinta Wilson. Ages, fourteen."

"Who are you?" I bared my teeth, forgetting my fear as it turned to defensiveness. Who was this melting summer snowman asking about my friends?

"That fire!" The man said like an old Baptist pastor. "It's that fire I see in you. That passion. How quickly did your fear fade as soon as I mentioned your friends?" The man stepped closer. His shadow stretched long and crooked across the ground.

My body broke its spell, and I could feel the blood rushing to my feet, allowing me to finally move. I tightened the rope around my fist, ready to use it as a weapon if I must. He won't take me without a fight.

The man laughed, popping out the sucker, his lips already stained red. "I'm just here to help you, Miss CeeCee. I mean no harm."

"You take one more step and I'll scream!"

The man threw up his hands in surrender or in praise, I couldn't tell. He waved them over his head, stepping backwards.

"Listen, I wanna make you an offer."

"Momma told me not to talk to strangers."

"And I agree with your momma. But here me out." He stuck the sucker into his mouth, chewed, then slid his hands in his pockets. "You want to win the Tallahatchie Double Dutch Competition, right?"

I narrowed my eyes.

He didn't wait for my answer.

"And I want you to win the competition. I can make that happen. I mean, you're a smart girl. With Evie's ankle, and Tasha's . . ."—he thought for a moment before the words tumbled out of his mouth—"everything else. We both know the trophy is as good as lost. And with it, New York. You on a huge stage in front of thousands, the crowd cheering your name, the chance to win and go on a Double Dutch tour outside the country. Everything you ever wanted rides on you."

Flashes of a cheering crowd, cameras rushing to interview us, me holding up the prize trophy all ran track in my mind.

I lower my fist.

My jaw clenched.

"So?" I said.

"So, let me help you."

"And how you gon' do that?"

"I just need one handshake and an itty-bitty tiny soul."

"Soul? You the Devil or something?"

"A devil isn't a who, it's more like a job title. Anyone can be a devil. Even you, Miss CeeCee."

"Well, I'm not making no deals with no devil."

He popped the sucker out of his mouth. Slobber stretched before it snapped.

My belly turned.

"You don't have to make the decision now. I'll be around. I mean, what's one tiny little soul when you can have the world, right?"

I gulped, biting my lower lip. "I'm out, creepy," I said, gripping my rope and putting a wide distance between us as I passed by.

"Just think about it!" He sounded too close as if he stood just over my shoulder, his voice right at my ear.

If I turned around, a smile of razor sharp teeth would bite me.

"She asked her mother, mother, mother for fifty cents, cents, cents, to see the elephants, elephants, elephants, jump over the fence, fence, fence . . ." His voice faded on the humid Mississippi wind.

I took off running, and didn't look back until I was home.

***

The competition was fierce. The Pepper Steppers had just exited the stage as the crowd gave a standing ovation. I bit my nails. My eyes darted to the shiny golden trophy sitting on the stand behind the DJ booth.

"We might as well go home," Tasha said. Her chubby jowls jiggled as she shook her head.

"We can't compare ourselves to the Pepper Steppers. Their family is a generation of ropers," Evie said.

"Man, look at that crowd. There are only two more teams before us. I'm positive we already lost. Plus, your ankle is still swollen." Tasha pointed at Evie's wrapped ankle.

"That's why, our good friend CeeCee, is going to bring it home for us, ain't that right?" Evie patted me on the shoulder.

I bit my index fingernail so low, I ripped into the cuticle.

Four women joined the stage behind the DJ booth and the crowd went quiet.

Everyone knew who they were. The Fantastic Four: Robin, Nikki, Delores, and De'Shone. When they were around my age, they won the Double Dutch World Championship in 1980. They traveled the world, performed in videos and commercials, and had spreads in magazines. They were who I wanted to be.

"Never give up! Keep going. Life has only just begun," Delores said as the crowd cheered.

Fire lit in my chest. A burning for something more, something greater than Tallahatchie, Mississippi. These women paved the way, and they will never be forgotten by history. I didn't want to be forgotten by history.

Tears dotted my cheeks. I turned into the crowd, heat clawing at my neck.

"Where you going?" Evie shouted behind me.

"I just need some water," I shouted back, almost tripping over my feet. I feared going on stage only to flop—The ropes tangling me like a cocoon, binding me in place as the crowd laughed. How could I be so scared and so hungry to win at the same time? It was paralyzing.

I pushed through the rambunctious crowd until I saw the stand with older women wearing pink plastic gloves and handing out fresh crisp water.

"Here you go, sugar," one auntie said with a smile that felt like a hug.

I gave a timid thank you and took the Styrofoam cup. I stepped off to the side, drank the water in two gulps, then threw the cup in the trash.

The DJ was already hyping the crowd up for the next team. Doubt snaking its way in. *We ain't gon' win.*

"They jumped so high, high, high . . ."

The stiff wind blew chills. Goosebumps pricked my skin.

"They reached the sky, sky, sky. And didn't come back, back, back. Till the 4th of July-ly-ly . . ." The voice oozed over me like molasses.

A red sucker dangled in my eyesight. I couldn't take my eyes off skeletal fingers and sharp nails holding the sucker. A scream swelled in my throat.

"Oh, no no no," he said, his chest hitting my back. "I'm only visible to you right now."

He rested his chin on my shoulder. I ripped myself away from him, bumping into a large Black man that reminded me of my uncle. "Hey," I said, pointing to the Devil. "You see him?"

The big man tilted his head at me, then his features grew sharp. "Somebody messing with you, who?" His eyes swept the crowd; most people carried drinks, nachos, hotdogs, and jump ropes.

The Devil was standing right in front of us, but nobody bumped into him. It was as if the crowd instinctively parted to make room.

I couldn't believe what I was seeing. He was in the mist of the crowd, a wide grin reaching from ear to ear, his skin detaching from his hairline. His black hair—oily and glistening.

I grabbed the big man's attention. "Sorry, my bad. I think I'm coming down with something. You know? The heat and everything."

The big man's face softened. "Make sure you keep yourself watered. Mess around and get heat stroke out here. Gon' back to yo' momma 'nem. If you need me, ask for Big John. We protect ours, okay?"

I nodded. Knowing he wouldn't be able to protect me from the Devil.

"Thank you," I said.

Big John gave one more look over, then he was gone. The crowd instinctively opened for him too.

"Awww, ain't that sweet," the Devil said.

"What you want?" I whisper–shouted.

The Devil undid the sucker's wrapper. "I came to see if you thought about our deal."

"I ain't selling my soul to no Devil."

"Never said it had to be your soul."

I blinked, watching him closely. His rotting teeth bled black as he bit into the candy. I would be dumber than two sloths changing a light bulb if I take anything he said seriously.

The crowd hooted and hollered as the announcer hyped up the Double Dutch team on stage. The jumper in the middle was doing pushups in beat with the ropes while executing every jump.

"This team will be hard to beat!" he said, as the DJ played explosion sound effects.

"I'm listening." I reluctantly gave in.

The Devil's eyes blinked vertically, his tongue split at the tip. "It could be anybody's soul. Somebody you love, somebody you hate." The Devil popped the sucker into his mouth. "It could even be anybody here in this crowd."

I twisted his words in my head, wringing them out like a soggy napkin. "If you don't want my soul. Then why is it important to make a deal with me? Just ask somebody else to do it."

The Devil shrugged. "I would, but you see there's certain requirements a candidate must meet. It's not like the good ole days, souls ripe with sin, ready to make a deal with any old crossroad demon." The Devil sighed.

"So, what requirements do I meet?"

The Devil bit into his candy. The crunch sounded like a skull crumbling.

"That's for me to know. You to find out. For right now . . ."—the Devil pointed to the stage as the team of girls finished—"your team is up next. I can give you what you want. All you have to do is say yes."

I bit my lower lip. Tumbled the thought in my mind. Looked at the crowd of strangers I would never see again. What was wrong with just picking a stranger? Their soul, not mine.

The Devil hummed the old Miss Mary Mack nursery rhyme.

"If I make this deal with you, then you agree that we will win this competition?"

"Agreed."

"In exchange for a soul that's not my own?"

"Absolutely."

The crowd was still cheering for a group that wasn't us. I wanted to shine. I wanted to beat the rest. The trophy had to be mine.

"Fine," I said.

The Devil held out his boney pale hand. "Deal."

Every nerve in my body was telling me no. I looked around, it seemed as if every back was turned from us. As if, somehow, we had made our own little funnel like the eye of a tornado. Whoever said there was peace in the center of a tornado, lied. Ain't nothing peaceful about being the next thing to be yanked into a world of chaos.

Hesitantly, I shook his hand. Wispy blue lines shot out of the palm of his hand up my arm. They were a cold river of ice, causing my entire body to tremble. "What's this?" I tried shaking off the creeping blue veins sinking into my skin.

A car salesman grin slithered across the Devil's face. The skin around his eyes dropped, his cheekbones were fine points, his eyes as dark as a muddy creek.

"Just a little insurance to our agreement. Once the contract is filled, you're free. Nice doing business with ya, Miss Celiah Marie Jackson." His hand slipped from mine, and then he was gone.

I blinked rapidly as if I had woken from a bad dream. I stumbled through the crowd, lost in my mind. My body was tingling, my vision smudging the crowd like watercolors. The music went dull in my ears.

Someone yanked at my arm. I jumped, ready to fight. I relaxed when I saw it was Evie and Tasha. I threw my arms around them and held them tight.

"Okay, girl. You aight?" Tasha said.

Evie scanned my face, worry etched in her brow.

"I'm okay," I said when I really wanted to scream *no!*

"You sure?" Evie bunched her lips in disbelief.

"Yeah. Just got a little mixed up, that's all."

"Mmm-hmm." Evie hummed. "Well, now is no time to be topsy-turvy. We got a show to perform."

The DJ mic scratched. "Now, coming to the stage, the Hop2it Magnolias!"

That was us. We scanned each other, nervously. Evie gave a comforting nod then rolled her ankle to check it. We ushered ourselves up the stairs; I tripped over my feet. Tasha caught me before I face planted.

All I could think was I hope to God the Devil gave me grace too. Tasha and Evie took their sides on each end of the rope.

One, two, one, two. Enter the loops with the foot closer to the ropes. I could do this. I jumped. High knees to the chest, and the rest was golden. My body took over. The ropes turned, and I didn't miss a beat. Not only did I jump, but I flipped. I have never done a flip before. My team was in sync. The crowd roared. Electricity sparked the stage with pure adrenaline.

I locked eyes with Tasha, she had a mischievous grin on her face. I knew exactly what she wanted to do before she even did it. Tasha, chubby Tasha from the block, flipped into the jump rope as I flipped out. She let go of the ropes as I caught them. The ropes didn't stop skipping once.

The crowd went ape shit!

Hoots and hollering, music blasting, drums went off in my right from a drumline I hadn't known was there. The DJ went wild on the mic. With a few more turns and tricks of the ropes, we finished to a crowd falling over themselves rooting us on. Cheering our name!

It wasn't a surprise when the DJ announced the winners for the full expense paid trip to New York to compete in the big leagues.

The Hop2it Magnolias. We won.

***

Three days went by and I was still high from the win. The first day, Tasha took the trophy home because that flip would be talked about for decades. Second day, Evie had it, and now the trophy sat on the mantel surrounded by my family's graduation pictures. My momma was so proud. "My baby is going to New York!" She took so many pictures of me.

In my room, surrounded by Omarion posters, I needed to see the trophy once again. Skipping down the stairs, sights set on the living room, a low hum of a deep voice flooded my ears.

"Miss Mary Mack, Mack, Mack..."

I froze, the blue veins glowing on my arms.

Was he supposed to come this soon? It's only been three days.

"All dressed in black, black, black . . ."

I eased around the corner to see a shadow materializing over my sleeping mother taking her Sunday afternoon nap.

"With silver buttons, buttons, buttons . . ." The Devil raised a pointed nail down the side of my momma's face. "All down her back, back, back . . ."

I swallowed my fear. "What are you doing here?" My voice trembled.

"To collect, Miss CeeCee."

"I'm not ready yet. I need more time"

"When rent is due, it's due." The shadow grew larger. Tendrils crawled along the floor like a fog machine switched on.

"Fine," I said, biting my lower lip. Thoughts of who I could choose rushed through my mind. "Take Mr. Easton." He was our crazy next-door neighbor. He yelled at everybody who came an inch close to his grass. He was going to hell anyway.

"No." The tendrils crept closer.

"That's who I choose. That is the deal," I said.

"The deal, Miss CeeCee was you can choose anybody's soul, but I get to choose if I accept it or not."

"That wasn't stated!"

"Not my fault you didn't read the fine print."

"There was no fine print. It was a verbal agreement." I panicked, my heart a hopping rabbit during hunting season.

"To-may-to, to-mah-to. A contract is a contract. You should have stated the clarifications when signing away a soul to a devil." He leaned over my momma. Her brown face rested peacefully as she breathed heavily. "Children never think of the consequences of their actions." Branch-like gnarled nails extended. "If you can't choose a soul I want, then I could just take your hard-working momma's." Spoiled milk fingers wrapped around my momma's throat.

"No!" I screamed.

My momma startled awake. "What? What?" She flipped around on the couch. "What's going on?"

The Devil had vanished.

"Noth-ing." I stuttered. "I thought I saw something."

Momma laid back on the pillow. "You need to see yourself outside. Disturbing my sleep. I swear."

"Sorry," I said, searching the living room, scanning the kitchen. The blinds were rolled up letting in the sun. No smokey tendrils covered the floor. I glanced at the trophy sitting on the mantel. "I'm so sorry," I whispered before rushing out of the house, hopping on my bike and speeding down the driveway.

I got myself into this, and I won't let the Devil hurt my momma. If he wanted me, he had to come chase me.

Every turn, I saw him—the Devil. Skin dripping as if it was melting face paint. He vanished and appeared on the side of the roads, in trees, in the shadows, but his voice was always right at my ear.

"She asked her mother, mother, mother for fifty cents, cents, cents, to see the elephants, elephants, elephants, jump over the fence, fence, fence . . ."

I raced down back streets trying to escape him—out to a dusty field, further away from my home.

"I want my soul, Miss CeeCee."

I scanned the road. No cars, no pickup trucks spotted. Nobody was walking or selling watermelons on the corner. I was alone. This wasn't supposed to happen like this. He tricked me.

"I gave you a soul like you asked," I cried through tears, pumping my bike pedals as hard as I could while dodging bushes and hard gravel. "This wasn't part of the deal!"

"I want my soul!" His voice boomed.

The oak trees blurred together.

"And I want it now!" He appeared in front of me, grabbing my handlebars, halting me. The back end of my bike flipped up, sending me flying off the seat and onto the empty street.

I scraped my knees and my arm had pebbles embedded into my skin. My entire body ached from impact.

"Whoa!" A familiar voice called. "Girl, you okay?"

I flipped around on my back to slowly sit up. Evie and Tasha were on their bikes, emerging from the woods we usually take to go to the corner store. They rushed my way.

"We were just coming over to see you," Tasha said, running to my side.

Tears blurred my vision. "I done messed up, y'all." I brought my knees to my chest and rocked.

"What are you talking about?" Evie checked my forehead.

"I did something bad."

"Girl, tell us!" Tasha demanded.

"We didn't win the competition on our own. I—" I inhaled before releasing. "I promised the Devil if he helped us win, I would give a soul to him."

The tension was thick. Tasha and Evie glanced at each other, but no laughter poured from their lips. Just silence. Eerie silence.

"Y'all think I'm crazy?" I dared to take a peek. Evie and Tasha were looking out to the road. Standing across the street was the Devil covered in black smokey tendrils, his face chalky, lips red, holding a sucker out to me.

"Is that the Devil?" Evie's voice was so low I almost couldn't hear her.

"You can see him?"

"How can I not?" Evie gulped.

Tasha kissed her teeth. "Dang, I knew that flip had to be supernatural. I ain't never flipped a day in my life."

"This is my fault," I wrestle to my feet. "I don't want y'all to be brought into this." I brushed pebbles off my arms and legs.

"You've already brought us into this." Tasha said, standing next to me.

"What is he doing?" Evie watched the Devil hold out the sucker with a cracked smile.

The Devil blinked out of existence and reappeared on the same side of the road we were on.

"Run!" I yelled.

We took off into the woods, hoping to cut through to the main road on the other side. But the woods never ended. I knew these trees, the grass, this same bush we passed three times like the back of my hand.

"Is it me, or are we going in circles?" Tasha broke the silence.

Panting, I searched the trees that blotted out the sun. Smokey tendrils weaved through the branches.

"What we gon' do?" Tasha grabbed my arm. "Where's Evie?" Tasha screamed. "Evie!"

I scanned the great oaks. She was just behind me.

"They jumped so high, high, high, they reached the sky, sky, sky . . ." The voice bounced off of every tree, amplified by echoes. The Devil hovered in the middle of the woods. Behind him was pitch black as if a wormhole began eating the trees. In his arms, he held Evie.

"Evie!" Tasha cried out.

This was all my fault. I wanted to win for us, and now I was going to lose it all. "I gave you what you wanted! You moved the goal post. You said I could choose any soul, and I chose! Let Evie go!"

The Devil laughed. "Such a silly little girl. You couldn't honestly believe that was all to it, could you?" The Devil slowly landed on the ground, floating forward. "Choose now, Miss CeeCee. Your soul or theirs?" His voice scattered across my skin like a batch of baby spiders. "If you can't choose. I will take them both!"

In a blink, Tasha was swooped up into the Devil's arms. Evie and Tasha's mouths were sewn shut around a sucker.

"You can't do this! You said one soul," I said.

"If you're in breach of contract, then I can take two souls. What will it be?"

I fell to my knees, my blue veins glowing. The lines pulsated, urging me to fulfill the contract. To choose. Pain shot through every muscle, causing my nerves to spasm as I fought hard against the impulse to give in. The Devil's greed flooded my mind, blocking me from thinking."

Choose, choose, choose! Give me a soul!

"Okay!" I yelled out. "I'll choose!" Air was wrung out of my lungs. "My soul. You can have my soul," I said. "Just please let them go."

The Devil grinned revealing a bloody red mouth like squashed tomatoes. Evie and Tasha both fought in his arms until the Devil dropped them on the ground. Evie managed to speak past the sucker in her mouth.

"No, just choose me. I'll give myself," she said.

Tasha, mouth still sealed shut, slapped her chest. *Me, choose me.* She seemed to say with her eyes.

My fear turned into rage.

I got my friends into this, and it will be me who gets them out.

The blue veins thrummed as the Devil came near. He held out a sucker, and I took it. That pleased him.

"Here, exactly what you asked for." I uncoiled the blue veins from my arms and willed them to take the essence of my soul. I handed a faint ghostly white light to him with anger etched in my brow.

"I knew you would eventually see it my way." The Devil turned the orb into his hand, and the blue veins faded away from my arms. Contract fulfilled.

"What is this?" He searched the orb until it expanded into its original shape.

"My sole," I said, watching the last of the blue veins vanish after giving him the sole of my shoe. A smirk played on my lips.

"No, no!" The Devil grew, towering over me.

"A contract is a contract. You asked and I gave." I stood my ground.

"I wanted a soul!"

"To-may-to, to-mah-to. You really should be more specific when verbalizing your contracts."

Tendrils whipped out of the Devil's body, heading straight toward Evie, Tasha, and me, but before they could curl around us, he stopped. His anger quickly sizzled. His shadows disappeared. It was as if someone had thrown ice on him. He was just a pale-faced man in a black suit.

He gave a light smile. "Devil work isn't what it used to be." He stared at me with glossy black eyes.

I held out the sucker. "Take it."

He took the white orb of the sole of my shoe and slid it into his pockets. "You will make a lovely little devil." He smiled. "Keep it. Miss Celiah Marie 'CeeCee' Jackson. Keep it until we meet again." The Devil faded with a tune. "Miss Mary Mack, Mack, Mack . . ."

The woods instantly became brighter. Evie and Tasha ran to me, their mouths unsealed.

"Don't you ever do anything like that!" Evie reprimanded.

Tasha spanked my butt. "Seriously, what the hell were you thinking!"

I held my besties close. Squeezing them with all my remaining strength.

"I was only thinking about winning. Not the people I could potentially hurt. I'm so sorry," I said.

Evie nodded. "No trophy's worth that."

Tears slipped down Tasha's cheek. "Even though that double backflip was bomb as hell."

We laughed as we held each other close, refusing to be the first to let the other go. The Tallahatchie Double Dutch trophy ended up in a dump truck. Later that summer, when we went to New York, we made sure we simply had fun, and that was enough.

E.A. Noble

E.A. Noble is an emerging speculative fiction author and poet. She is passionate about centering Queer, fat, neurodivergent, Black, and POC characters. She crafts stories that challenge the norms and celebrates underrepresented voices. Her debut fantasy, "When Blood Meets Earth" won an

Indie Literary Award for best fantasy. Completed works, visit theeajournal.me.

The Closet Window
Lori Titus

Now that some time has passed, I think I can talk about it. I was only a little girl at the time. Five years old with pigtails, brown skin, and round eyes. Back then, Mama was maybe thirty-two, seven years younger than I am today. She was curvy and pretty, with black wavy hair. She wore glasses and dresses that skimmed above her knees. My older sister Caroline was sixteen and looked like Mama's younger twin. That was long before Sis met her husband or had any of her four sons.

Mama had so many sayings, but the one that stands out in my memory: Look for things in the dark spots where you can't see.

Caroline and I grew up in the house that our grandparents had bought. A white house with a green roof. The backyard stretched out a half-acre, surrounded by ancient oaks. There were two bedrooms when they first bought the house, then grandpa added a third room onto the back so that his son and daughter would each have their own. Mama kept the house after my grandparents moved away. The room in the back, the smallest room, was Caroline's when she was little. When I was born, it became mine.

The room was simple. Wood floors. A nightstand on the right-hand side of the double bed. A white porcelain lamp painted with pale pink roses. There wasn't a dresser, just an armoire. And then there was the closet.

The closet faced my bed. The door to the closet had an old-fashioned crystal knob. It was the only one left in the house like that. When you opened it, there was a little window inside the top of the closet. That used to be the back door, with the top section of the glass cut into curved thirds. One morning, I pushed aside my clothes and let my fingers trace the lines where the door used to be, which was plastered over on the inside. It was secured on the outside with cement, Mama said. No one could get through.

If you left the closet door open, you could see the tops of the trees swaying in the backyard. I used to like watching the rain come down in the afternoon through that sliver of window.

At night, when the blue porchlight was on, there was something about looking through that glass that was spooky. Especially when the wind was blowing, and the trees swayed, their limbs long and twisted. I made sure that I closed the closet door every night before bed.

I don't know when I started to feel that I was being watched, or that the closet door needed to remain closed to keep someone away. I went from being very comfortable in my room to not wanting to be in there, even to play with my dolls.

"It's always cold, Mama," I said one day. We were sitting around the kitchen table, having breakfast. The kitchen, decorated in shades of pale yellow and cream, always felt like the brightest and safest place in our home. Sundays were when we had a big breakfast: grits, eggs, toast, smothered potatoes. Coffee for Mama and my sister, orange juice for me.

Mama and Caroline shared a glance. It was gone quickly.

"It shouldn't be *that* cold this time of year, Naomi. It's almost Spring. We can put a space heater in there."

The space heater coils glowed red in the dark but didn't warm the room. I'd had it for maybe a week when the thing flickered out. Mama promised to buy me a new one when she got paid. She was irritated that it had stopped working. She said it had only lasted one, maybe two winters.

Sometimes, when I went into my room in the middle of the day, I'd find the closet door open. I told myself maybe Mama or Caroline had opened it. I didn't ask them because I was afraid they would say they hadn't bothered. And if they didn't, what would that mean?

I slammed the closet door shut and left the room. I hated that I had to return at bedtime.

I remember walking across the wood floor, the slats sighing under my small weight. It was so much colder in that room than anywhere else in the house. Mama put more layers on my bed, including a thick white comforter that made it hard to turn very much. I clutched it, my hands filled with handfuls of knobby fabric. There were fringes around the edge; sometimes I twirled them between my fingers. I laid on my back and stared at the ceiling. A nightlight in the hallway offered a dim yellow glow that came no closer than the open bedroom door.

My eyes were heavy. I was about to turn over when I happened to look at the closet door. It stood wide open. I froze. Should I get up and close it? That seemed like a dangerous proposition. I couldn't see anything in the dark space of the closet. I felt eyes watching me.

I didn't move. I barely breathed. Seconds turned into minutes. I could hear the clock ticking in the hallway.

Eventually, I got sleepy again. I told myself that maybe there wasn't anything there. My eyes closed.

I'm not sure what woke me exactly, but when I looked again, something was wrapped around the brass footboard of my bed. A hand, a gnarled hand. Or something more like a claw. I looked up, not wanting to see. My body shook.

He was a man, or something shaped like a man. A shadowy dark figure. This was something tall, with arms and legs too long and misshapen in a way that suggested this thing had never been human. The face—mouthless, eyeless, feature-less—was the most frightening thing. How could I feel this thing staring at me without it even having the space for eyes?

I screamed.

Mama told me later that she brought me to her room to sleep, and that even then I hadn't slept until the first rays of light pushed up against the windowsill.

"Child, what did you see?" Mama asked. "That was a blood-curdling scream. Don't tell me that was no night-mare."

I didn't want to tell her. It sounded crazy. We were in the kitchen again, where everything seemed so normal and peaceful. The smell of bacon and toast that would usually make my stomach grumble made me feel sick.

Caroline told me how both she and Mama had ran to my room in the middle of the night, finding me screaming and hysterical. It explained why my throat was sore. Between their prodding and Mama's frowning silence, I told them what I had seen.

My mother just shook her head. Caroline stared at me.

"Mama," my sister finally said. "I never told Naomi about seeing the dark man when I was little."

"Naomi can sleep in my room," Mama said. She got up from the table. She went to the cabinet and retrieved a bowl. I predicted from the ingredients she pulled from the fridge that she was about to make pancakes. "At least until we can sell this place and move."

Lori Titus

Lori Titus is a writer who loves fantastic and scary things.

Deadly Visions
Vivienne Neal

Speculations as to what really happened to Betty and James Bey were circulating throughout the community. Rumor had it that James ran off with his paramour, Pootsie Brown. Neighbors saw Pootsie as a woman who had the morals of an alley cat and could not hold a candle to Betty. Before long, Betty also disappeared without a trace. The town criers could not understand what Betty saw in James, who had the physical traits of an imp. Betty was beautiful, stood 5'9" tall, and could have been a runway model for any high-fashion designer.

Betty, seen as a sweet and loving wife, was clueless when it came to her husband's infidelity. The community imagined she left town after learning about his betrayal. They believed that healing her shattered heart was her main goal, but that was far from the truth. If people knew what occurred in that empty brownstone and the co-op where Pootsie lived, they would have concluded that an evil entity had taken over those two dwellings, which remain vacant to this day.

****

While cleaning the bathroom mirror, the reflection of her dead husband James frightened Betty. It was a momentous day because it was St. Valentine's Day when she saw his image. The holiday was always a memorable day. Couples packed City Hall, got married, and vowed to honor, love, and be faithful to each other till death do them part, or as James's deceased mother once told her son, "until something better comes along." Unfortunately, James took his mother's words to heart, because something better did come his way, and her name was Pootsie Brown. Unlike James, Betty took her vows seriously. But soon, a day of reckoning would descend on James and his lover.

One year after their marriage, Betty discovered a deed to a lavish one-bedroom apartment in a sixteen-story co-op in

Stuyvesant Heights, a prosperous community in Brooklyn, New York. Thinking the gift was for her, she was ready to celebrate by planning an elaborate trip. To her dismay, James bought the unit as a gift for his paramour, Pootsie Brown. When Betty discovered that James was cheating on her, she started to plan for James and his mistress's demise.

While preparing lunch for James, Betty added a powerful sleep-inducing drug to his food. After consuming the meal, he fell asleep. With a hatchet, she removed his head. She chopped the cranium and carcass into bite-sized chunks. She then placed the remnants into a huge pressure cooker until they were soft enough to make a tasty cuisine for their Siamese cat, Cid. After cleaning up the spattered blood, Betty admired her work and was ready to tackle her next task.

The next day, a blissful Betty searched high and low for the key to Pootsie's unit, but she had no luck in finding it. She went to that co-op, took the elevator to Pootsie's third-floor unit, and jimmied the lock with a large bobby pin, something she learned with a quick internet search. Without a hitch, she was able to unlock the door. She searched the unit and found Pootsie napping on an antique rocking chair in the den. Betty removed the same axe she used on James from her canvas bag and hacked off the head of his lover. She then put the skull into a black plastic bag and sealed it with duct tape. Betty carried the sack down the back stairwell, exited the co-op, and placed it into a dumpster behind the complex. Eventually, waste management discarded the bag.. No one was the wiser as to what was in it.

A day later, Betty returned to the co-op, chopped what was left of Pootsie's corpse, placed the remains into a large flowerpot, concealed it all with planting soil, and placed the pot on the terrace. With an industrial cleaning solution, Betty washed off the bloodstains from the chair, walls, and floor. She left the area flawless, as though no butchery had ever taken place. Eventually, the flowerpot bloomed with vibrant flowers, pollinated by robins, bees, and butterflies— a great selling point for anyone with a green thumb who wanted to buy that unit.

Betty fulfilled her job. *I killed two snakes with one hatchet.* She would never have to explain to the neighbors what happened to her husband or his trifling lover. Since Betty, James, and Pootsie lost contact with their family and had no close friends, no one would miss them. Betty was planning to leave New York soon. She would not have to file a missing person report with the police department. If anyone asked, she would just say, "He probably ran off with his mistress."

One month later, James's likeness appeared a second time on a mirror positioned behind the sofa in the living room of their two-story brownstone, two blocks from Pootsie's co-op. But something eerie happened. He started to fade. Hissing sounds from their cat Cid startled Betty. When she turned to see the cat's uproar, the feline transformed into a poltergeist. Suddenly, a large spider was crawling up the mirror. Betty was even more alarmed. Spiders never appeared in their home, even though waterbugs and pesty red ants were a constant problem.

Yet, Betty was about to face a day of reckoning for her crimes. Cid took on the image of her husband, James. The spider transformed into his mistress, Pootsie, who injected Betty with venom that would forever trap her in a cobweb, eventually turning her into dust.

From that day forward, James and Pootsie continued to declare their love for each other, living happily ever after in that brownstone.

Vivienne Neal

Vivienne Neal is a writer, blogger, and an author. She is a storyteller with a wicked sense of humor, has been writing articles for over forty years and started penning fictional short stories in 2007, getting her story ideas from observing people, places, and things and watching TV court cases.

The Mystery of Shepherd's Pie
C.Y. Marshall

The news that morning was the same the town of Clivesdale had heard in the last two months. Headlines read in bold black letters, **"Two More Children Missing."** Panic was an understatement of what the townspeople were feeling. It was more like dread and fear. An ominous blanket of darkness had covered the town, and no one knew how to fix it. The sheriff, who walked around with concern on his face, was just as clueless as everyone else as to what was happening. Most times he tried to camouflage his liquor with coffee, but everyone knew what was in his thermal. You could tell not only from his glassy eyes with dilated pupils, but the smell that came from his pores was just as telling. No amount of cheap cologne could cover the scent of cheap liquor.

Sheriff Tupperman pulled up to the Clive Home for Abandoned Children. His stomach somersaulted as he looked at the massive concrete structure. Memories flooded his mind like an old black and white movie of his mother dropping him off there as a child. "I just need some time, my little cowboy. I . . . I uh, get sick sometimes and it feels like the walls are closin' in on me, you know? But I'm going away so I can get better. Then I'll come get you and we can bake a three-layer chocolate cake, eat ice cream, and watch old westerns. How does that sound, cowboy?" The memory was as vivid as the day it happened. Sheriff Tupperman finished his spiked coffee and put two pieces of peppermint candy in his mouth. He took a deep breath and got out of his cruiser. As usual, there were reporters outside the children's home swarming like flies over shit to get the latest story. They rushed towards him like a pack of angry wolves shouting questions and snapping pictures.

"Do you have any leads, Sheriff?"

"Who's kidnaping the children, Sheriff?"

"Have you questioned the lady living out in the woods in that old house yet?"

"Do you think the children are dead?"

"Why are the children from the home going missing?"

Reporters continued to yell questions, sounding like a bad choir out of sync. Sheriff Tupperman raised his hands as if directing the choir and said, "Listen please." It became silent and everyone looked at him with anxiousness, waiting for what he had to say.

"Right now, I have no answers to your questions. However, we are actively looking at some leads from tips we were given. We are working hard to find out what happened to the children. When we know, you'll know. So, for now, that's all I have."

The reporters yelled out questions again as the sheriff walked away, but one question stopped him cold in his tracks. He turned around to a woman standing behind the reporters. She had no little device in her hand to record information or a camera to take pictures. He did not think she was a reporter, so who was she? Sheriff Tupperman cleared his throat and walked towards the woman. He stopped some feet in front of her and asked, "What did you say?"

The woman, standing poised and wearing a long black wool coat with a fur collar, a black fascinator hat with a veil and a fur black muff softly said, "Is the old lady the reporters refer to living in the woods the eater of children? Has she returned?" The reporters, scurrying to take out their pads and pens, while others held up their recording devices, looked to Sheriff Tupperman for an answer.

"Uh, ma'am, as I said, we have no answers as of yet but we're working on it."

"But you do have your answers. She's back like she said. You know who she is. I'm sure you remember. Don't you, Sheriff?"

Sheriff Tupperman smiled nervously as the reporters looked to him for answers. He vaguely remembered what she spoke about, but it felt familiar. It felt like something he should remember; something that was a part of him, but what?

"Sheriff, who is the eater of children?" one reporter yelled.

"Is the old lady a murderer?" the other yelled.

"Who said they were coming back?"

The woman turned away humming a tune that sent a bolt of chills through Sheriff Tupperman. "I'll make you plump. I'll make you ripe. I'll peel your skin and eat you tonight."

She walked away as the reporters followed behind her yelling questions. Sheriff Tupperman walked over near a tree and bent over. He began to cough violently and threw up the spiked coffee he drank. Like a memory that had been locked away in the deepest, darkest part of the psyche, the chain had been removed, and the memory was open for him to view. Now he remembered.

.⁺ ·₊)○(₊·⁺ ·*

Sheriff Tupperman entered the Clive Home for Abandoned Children and stood in the hallway to further compose himself. The mysterious woman had unleashed memories that he thought he had hidden safely away. The stories he heard as a child to scare him were true. For now, he could not think about her or what he was feeling. The disappearance of the six children took precedence over any childhood urban legend.

The Home was silent except for a few voices that came from the office. With all the children who lived there, he could never understand why the sounds of laughter did not fill the halls and rooms. Although the children there longed for a family to take them away, to love them and care for them, he imagined that was when there would be laughter. Sheriff Tupperman made his way to the office to speak with Director Peddleton. She was a stern woman with a rigid face that never smiled. She spoke through her teeth and always looked over the rim of her glasses that sat on the tip of her nose. There was nothing that said softness or kindness about her.

"Have you found out who's kidnapping my children, Sheriff?" she asked.

"No, but we're working hard on it."

"Is this a repeat of 1965 when the children went missing and the only thing found was their clothing in the woods?"

"Uh, I don't really remember that too much," he said softly.

"I guess you wouldn't really remember that much. After all, you were just a kid then. I would assume you blocked it out. Or maybe the adults didn't talk about it around you. Whatever the case, it's happening again. Children are going missing from my Home, and no one is doing anything about it. Have you checked the house in the woods?"

"Yes, and there's nothing there."

"What about the old lady?"

"She's harmless. She can barely move. And besides, no one ever sees her. As far as I'm concerned, there is no one living out there. Anyway, can I see the room of the girls who went missing?"

Ms. Peddleton looked at him over her glasses before standing up and retrieving the room key from the hook of which it hung upon. "Follow me," she said, walking out of the office. She walked with a quick stride as the heels of her black shoes made a thunderous sound in the quiet halls. Sheriff Tupperman hurried behind her as he looked in the bedrooms where the doors were open. The children in the rooms sat quietly on their beds with a book in their hands. When they would hear the sound of feet walking by, they would look up with a blankness in their eyes. He would smile and they would lower their heads, expressionless.

Ms. Peddleton stopped in front of a door with the names Zora and Toni on it. She rattled the large ring of keys to find the correct one. When she found it, she put it in the keyhole and grunted as she opened it. Sheriff Tupperman forgot how enormous and heavy the bedroom doors were. He looked around at the immaculate room. It looked as if no one ever lived there. There was no sign of a room where little girls lived. No dolls. No toys. No pink matching bed sets. Just narrow twin beds with gray blankets and white pillows. Sheriff Tupperman searched around, opening the closet and dresser drawers. All signs that anyone lived there were gone.

"Where are their clothes? Their belongings?' he asked.

"All packed away in the storage room in the basement. We may need this room. We can't hold onto it forever. As much as we want them to come back, business is still business."

"I see. And when was the last time you saw them?

"Thursday evening, two days ago. It was after dinner, and they were acting strange. They were sitting in the playroom on the floor, facing each other, and they were singing that awful song."

"What song?"

"You remember. Uh, it says, I'll make you plump. I'll make you ripe. I'll peel your skin and eat you tonight."

Sheriff Tupperman's heart dropped. Something was definitely strange, and he had a foreboding feeling that he would find out very soon what it was.

⁺ ·₊))○((₊· ⁺ ·⁺

On the ride home the Sheriff began to remember bits and pieces of the song and the old lady who supposedly kidnapped children to eat them. He always believed it was a folktale to scare children into doing the right thing or doing what you wanted them to do. However, he did remember how children started disappearing from the Home. At first, he thought they were the lucky ones to be chosen by a loving family, but as time went on, he realized they weren't so lucky. To this day, sixty years later, no trace or evidence of them has ever been found.

Sheriff Tupperman pulled into his driveway and sat, thinking. If children were being kidnapped primarily from the Home during that time, why would his mother take him there? Why would she leave him in such a place? Too many memories and thoughts came rushing to him and he needed to slow it down. He didn't want coffee. He wanted a stiff drink. The Sheriff got out of his cruiser and walked to his front door. The air had turned piercing cold, and the wind played an unholy melody. He turned to look across the barren field, and thought, for a moment, he saw children standing there watching him. Some were dressed like they used to when he was a child and the others were dressed from the current time. In front of them were the two recent missing girls, Zora and Toni. Sheriff Tupperman shook his head and blinked his eyes repeatedly, believing his mind was playing tricks on him and he was seeing things. After doing that a few times, they were still there.

"Hey," he yelled, hurrying towards them.

The children laughed as they sang, "She made us plump. She made us ripe. She peeled our skin and ate us each night."

Sheriff Tupperman rushed towards the field as the children laughed and ran, disappearing into the frigid wind. He stopped and kneeled while holding his knees and trying to catch his breath. The Sheriff did not know what he had just witnessed but it had him flustered and scared. He inched back to his house, turning around a few times to see if what he saw was real. There was nothing there.

The Sheriff opened the door to his house and walked inside. He did not realize there was an envelope on the floor as he slammed the door behind him and hurried to the kitchen. Quickly opening the bottle of tequila on the table, he gulped some before slamming the bottle down while making a loud grunt. The tequila burned his chest as he stumbled back against the sink, wiping his mouth with the back of his hand. He picked up the bottle and repeated the same ritual before walking into his living room, bottle in hand.

As he was about to sit down, he noticed the envelope. He picked it up and read the front, feeling like the wind had been knocked out of him. There was no return address, just his name on the front; a name he had not seen or heard in over sixty years. In big, bold, black letters, the name **STEPHEN "COWBOY" TUPPERMAN** was neatly written. He sat down, drank the rest of the tequila in the bottle, and stared at the envelope.

"Stephen Cowboy Tupperman," he mumbled. The only person who called him "Cowboy" was his mother, the woman he never saw again after being dropped off at the Home. No one else knew his nickname because he did not want to share it with anyone. That was something special and only reserved for his mother to call him. He gently turned over the envelope and lifted the clasp that kept it closed. His heart felt like someone was inside his chest beating it like a drum. The pulsations were quick and rapid. Small beads of sweat began to form on his forehead and his hands trembled, as he felt the moisture from his sweaty palms. His chest started to heave up and down while his breathing became erratic. He knew he needed to calm down but he could not.

Sheriff Tupperman retrieved newspaper clips out the envelope, cut out headlines and pictures. He sat forward in his chair and placed all the items on the coffee table in front of him. The newspaper articles dated back to 1965, with some of the shocking headlines screaming in all caps, "ARE THE CHILDREN DEAD," "ANOTHER CHILD DISAPPEARS" "THE CURSE OF CLIVESDALE HOME FOR ABANDONED CHILDREN," and "MISSING CHILDREN: IS THE URBAN LEGEND TRUE?"

Sheriff Tupperman searched the articles and pictures trying to see if anything would jump out in importance. He had no clue who left the envelope or why. As he continued to look through the pictures, he noticed one of a woman standing outside of the Clivesdale Home next to the same tree where he vomited earlier. He stared hard at the picture trying to see it clearly as he brought it closer to his eyes. Sheriff Tupperman gasped loudly, dropped the newspaper article, and sat startled back in his chair. He did not know if his eyes were playing tricks on him from the tequila or he was hallucinating. It seemed as if the wind howled louder and blew harder, giving him a sinister feeling. Without hesitation, he got up, grabbed his jacket and keys, and headed outside.

.⁺ .₊)◯(₊.⁺ .

An overcast had taken the sun away, making the ride to the old lady's house in the woods more eerie. Sheriff Tupperman had not been totally honest with the townspeople or reporters. He nor his deputies had gone out to the house in the woods to check it out. He felt there was no need to. One thing he did remember about the missing children's case when he was a child was that they had accused the woman living in the house in the woods of kidnapping and murdering them. He remembered seeing her one day, then the next she was gone. The town rejoiced and life got back to normal.

He figured if she were still living there, she would be too old

to do anything, particularly kidnap children.

Sheriff Tupperman turned down the winding road to the

house. With all the trees and overgrown bushes, it was hard

to see the house beyond it. He pulled close to the house and

parked his cruiser. It actually seemed abandoned as if no

one lived there. The only thing that proved that wrong was

the smoke coming from the chimney. Sheriff Tupperman got

out of the cruiser and had the most haunting feeling. He

felt like something awful was about to happen or had hap-

pened. Whatever was drawing him there, he had to find out

what happened to the children. The sheriff carefully walked

around the outside of the house. As he walked around, he

saw several old dolls and toy trucks on the ground. He bent

down to pick up the truck because it resembled one he had

as a kid. It was obvious the toys were incredibly old and had

not been played with in a long time. Things were getting

stranger by the minute. Sheriff Tupperman walked to the

front door, still holding the truck, and knocked. He knocked several more times before turning the knob to the door. It made a loud squeaky sound as he slowly opened it and stuck his head inside.

"Hello, it's Sheriff Tupperman. Is anyone home?" he asked, opening the door more. "Hello, it's the Sheriff. I'm coming in."

When he walked inside the house, he was surprised to see how nice it was. He expected to see a dilapidated home that was unfit for habitation, but it was the total opposite. Surprised by what he saw, the sheriff stood there for a few seconds, wondering if what he was looking at was real. He was not sure about anything, especially after seeing the children and the pictures. The house had a sweet smell, like baked apple pies. It was warm and extremely neat, as if someone were expecting company. Sheriff Tupperman slowly walked around the house, examining all the knick-knacks displayed on the oak mantle and coffee tables.

Although the house gave warmth from the cold, it also gave the sheriff an uneasy feeling. In his gut, something did not feel right. He continued through the house and came across the kitchen. There was a large pot cooking on the stove. The steam rising from it indicated it had been cooking for a while. Sheriff Tupperman walked over to it and slowly peeked inside. It was beef stew. On the large island in the kitchen were potatoes, carrots, and meat. To the left of him was a huge oven. He had never seen such a huge oven in a house. If there was an old lady that lived here, why would she need such a massive oven? Being curious, he walked over to it and opened it. There were six trays inside that were filled with pie. The sheriff became increasingly curious, but nervous.

As he closed the oven, he heard the floorboard above him creaking, and then he heard children's laughter. He walked out of the kitchen over to the stairs and yelled, "who's up there?" There was no answer, only giggles. Sheriff Tupperman began up the stairs and the children sang, "She made us plump. She made us ripe. She peeled our skin. She's going to eat us tonight."

The sheriff put his hand on his gun holster and unfastened it. He would never shoot a child, but he did not know what awaited him up the stairs. He tip-toed up the stairs, with his heart beating fast and his legs trembling. He could still hear laughter and the singing of the song, but he saw no one.

"Alright, come out here now. This is not a game. Where are you?"

The laughter grew more intense and louder as he made his way down the hall. Each room he passed had three neatly made-up beds. The situation grew more strange and eerie by the minute. As he slightly turned the hallway, there was a closed room door at the end. In front of the door stood the children he saw earlier in the field. Sheriff Tupperman's heart dropped. He blinked his eyes repeatedly, wondering if they would disappear. They laughed uncontrollably as the Sheriff suffered nausea. The laughter did not sound like children's laughter anymore, but something far more sinister. It made him stumble back against the wall and cover his ears.

As the laughter continued to fill the house with a covering of darkness, the door to the bedroom opened. The laughter suddenly stopped and one by one the children vanished. Sheriff Tupperman fumbled to retrieve his gun, but something would not let him.

"Now, now Cowboy. No need for that," the woman suddenly said.

He was terrified as he tried to make sense of what was happening and who was standing in front of him. It could not be. How could it be?

"Who are you? Where are the children?"

"Why Sheriff, they're everywhere," she said with a chuckle.

"You? You were the lady at the Home this morning asking questions. And not only that, I've seen you before."

"Well of course you've seen me before, Cowboy." She laughed.

"How do you know my nickname? No one knows that but my mother and she has been gone for a long time."

"Oh, really?" she mysteriously asked.

"This can't be real. I saw you in a picture from years ago and you looked exactly the same. What trick are you playing and where are the children?"

The woman, still dressed in her long black wool coat with a fur collar, a black fascinator hat with a veil, and a fur black muff, smiled the most evil, deranged smile he had ever seen. She started towards him but when he looked closely, he could see she was not walking but floating. Sheriff Tupperman's eyes widened as he continued to reach for his gun, but he could not get it. The sound of laughter from the children started again, then they began singing the song.

The Sheriff backed up quickly, trying to make his way back to the steps but he fell. He closed his eyes and tried to yell but nothing came out. When he opened them, things looked different. The time was different. As he tried to regain his composure, he heard the most beautiful, angelic voice he had not heard in over sixty years. Sheriff Tupperman stood up and followed the voice. The house seemed familiar, and he remembered it was his childhood home. When he found where the voice was coming from, he saw his mother sitting in the kitchen talking to a woman. The woman's back was towards him, and he could only see his mother's face. She was crying and pleading with the woman. Sheriff Tupperman slowly walked over to the table. As the woman's face was revealed, he could sense a dreadful and dark aura coming from her. It was the same woman from the pictures and the house in the woods. Her appearance had not changed.

"Please, don't kill my Cowboy," his mother pleaded.

"Of course not. If you give me what I want, I will spare his life. Always."

"You promise?" his mother tearfully asked.

"I promise. Just take him to Clivedales Home for Abandoned Children and as promised, he will live."

Sheriff Tupperman's mother cried as the tears flowed heavily down her face. The woman sat with an evil grin tapping her long fingers on the table. She picked up her cup, drank the rest of her tea, and sat it down.

"Okay, stop crying. I need your body to be free from stress. It will make the transition smoother. After you take your son to the home, come back and we will seal our deal. Your body for your son's life."

Sheriff Tupperman gasped loudly as he sat up on the floor. The woman was sitting in a chair surrounded by the children who went missing over the years. He scooted backwards and leaned against the wall.

"What are you? What did you do to my mother?" he tearfully asked.

"Well, I am your mother. I'm using her body. Living for as long as I do, after years I need another body, and your mother was so gracious to give me hers. I may look different, Cowboy, but I'm still your mother."

"Why did you make my mother give me up?" he asked as he started to cry.

"Aren't you listening? I needed another body. Besides, I have always watched over you and protected you. Every time I took another child to grind them up, I spared you."

"Why children? Why kidnap and murder children?"

"Because they make the best Shepherd's Pie. If you cook them down long enough, their skin will be nice and tender. It makes the grinding easier. Then you can make anything you want. I like to use other parts of them too. Children are just tasty. MmmMmm, so good."

"I have to arrest you. I have to take you in."

The woman laughed a hearty laugh as she stood up and walked over to him. She kneeled beside him and rubbed her hand over his cheek. Sheriff Tupperman gazed in her eyes, and he thought for a moment they were his mother's eyes. His heart sank and he felt like the little boy she dropped off at the home many years ago. He knew he couldn't arrest her or take her in. "She" was not a "she" but an "evil being." She would never be his mother, and he would never be able to stop her.

Sheriff Tupperman stood up and focused on her. He backed away as the children started singing again. Something felt different about the song and the house. The woman sat back down as the children surrounded the Sheriff. Terror invaded his body as he tried to get away from them, but he was paralyzed with fear.

"Sheriff, I was thinking. I want something meatier to eat tonight. Are you up for the plucking?" She laughed as he screamed and the children began tearing him apart.

✦ ☽◯☾ ✦

A month had passed since the disappearance of Sheriff Tupperman. Rumors spread that he left because the pressure of not finding the children was too much. When the other deputies searched his home, it had been cleaned out. There was no trace that anyone ever lived there. His disappearance was definitely a mystery.

Sheriff Baskerman, the new sheriff, sat behind his desk and read the latest article of a missing child.

"NO LEADS. JUST MISSING CHILDREN."

As he sat feeling dismayed, the door to the town's police station opened and a well-dressed woman walked in. She stood at the counter as Sheriff Baskerman got up and walked out of his office to her.

"Yes, may I help you?'

"Yes. I was wondering are there any leads in the missing children's cases?"

"I am not at liberty to say but we are working night and day to find the children."

"Well, have you checked the house in the woods where the old lady lives?"

"Yes, we have and there's nothing there. Like I said ma'am, we're doing everything we can. We appreciate your concern, but we have it covered."

"I still think you should check the old house, but I understand. Oh, before I forget," she said, taking a casserole dish out of her bag and setting it on the counter. "I made some stew a while ago. I took it out of my freezer and warmed it up nice and hot today. I figured you and your deputies would like to have a nice hot meat. It's from an old recipe; one you may find familiar."

"That's truly kind of you. Thank you," he said, raising the dish to his nose and smelling it. "Smells good. I can't wait to get a big bowl of it."

"Enjoy," she said. Turning to walk out as she sang, "I'll make you plump. I'll make you ripe. I'll peel your skin and eat you tonight."

"Hey, what's that you're singing?" the Sheriff asked, feeling the hair stand up on the back of his neck.

"Oh, it's just a song I've been singing forever. Enjoy your stew," she said, walking out of the town's police station with her phantom children waiting in the wind.

C.Y. Marshall

I am an avid horror lover and writer who enjoys writing stories that evokes fear . Being the author of eight books my stories range from female serial killers to blood sucking

vampires. Get lost in one of my books and familiar with the

characters. They are waiting to become your friend.

Clean, Miranda, Clean
N.M. Chaney

As the rain silently falls to the ground, Miranda bites into a ripe juicy plum and continues to think about what to do next. She aimlessly paces back and forth. The stillness outside is in stark contrast to what is happening inside her mind. She wonders if she went outside would the silence rub off and put her mind at ease.

"Snap out of it," she thinks to herself.

It would only be a matter of time before they arrived and would undoubtedly want to know what happened. Would this be a case of guilty until proven innocent or would they genuinely be interested in what she had to say?

Chills course through her veins as she looks over at the lifeless body sprawled out on the living room floor. She didn't mean to kill him. She just got carried away, that's all. At least the evening started on a good note, she shrugs as she takes another bite of her plum. Her mind wanders back in time.

She was elated when Logan asked her to come to his parents' cabin for the weekend. They had been dating for about a year and she had just met them. The admiration was mutual. Logan was an only child and his parents spoiled him silly. He grew up to become a decent human being who didn't feel as if the world revolved around him.

Miranda was the younger of two kids. She had an older brother Jake who had been incarcerated for the past two years. He wouldn't be eligible for parole for another two years. Miranda couldn't care less. They weren't all that close. He'd always been in and out of jail. It's as if she hardly knew him. She loved her family even though she didn't feel it was reciprocated. Her father passed away a year ago and her mom hadn't been the same since. He was their foundation and with him gone, the foundation was weak.

When Logan approached her in the produce section at Trader Joe's, it totally caught her off guard. She loved plums and had like five bucks in her pocket. Why not buy five dollars worth of plums? They were her comfort food. She ate them whenever she felt stressed, although she never really needed a reason to eat a plum. He wanted to get to know her better, so he asked her out on a date. She agreed and their first date was a picnic in the park.

A loud knocking at the front door cuts Miranda's day-dreaming short.

"Who is it?" she cautiously asks.

No answer. She walks a little closer to the door and asks louder "Who is it?" Again, no answer. While trying to decide whether to open it, another loud knock startles her. She opens the door and can't help but laugh at what she sees on the other side. She almost feels foolish for being so panicky and letting her thoughts get the best of her.

She's staring at a young guy holding two pizza boxes and enjoying music on his iPod. No wonder he didn't hear her. Once he sees Miranda, he pulls out the ear plugs. "Uh, that'll be twenty dollars, Ma'am" as he searches for the receipt.

"You have the wrong address," she tells him.

"Shit man. I hate when that happens," he says. "Sorry about that."

"Don't worry about it," she says and shuts the door.

She looks in the peephole and chuckles to herself as she watches this guy fumble around. He finally composes himself, sticks his ear plugs back in, and disappears.

Miranda must act fast. The next knock may be someone far more dangerous than a pizza delivery guy. Her eyes scan the cabin from the blood stains to the body, to the messy living room. She jumps into cleanup mode and Operation Bleach is underway.

She decides to tackle the body first. She begrudgingly starts the laborious task of dragging Logan into the bathroom. He is so heavy. She pauses and takes a sip of her red plum juice and continues to drag him into the bathroom. Once there, she pushes, pulls, tugs, and flips him until he is face up in the bathtub.

With the heavy lifting out of the way, she goes to the closet in the hallway, grabs a pair of sunshine yellow gloves, walks into the kitchen, then pulls a meat cleaver out of the drawer. Back in the bathroom, she grabs a ratty house robe hanging on the back of the door. She takes another long swallow of her juice and gets to work.

The body is wearing blue jeans, a black belt, and a crisp white Oxford button-up shirt. He has on a pair of traditional brown boat shoes with no socks. She strips him of his clothes and throws them to the side. Everything he wore was soiled with blood and torn flesh. Once he was completely naked, she could see the damage she inflicted. With each gash through his skin. He resembled a pig carcass on a hook in a meat shop.

The usually great smelling cologne he wore reeked when mixed with the aroma of blood and mutilated flesh. She grabs the cleaver, lifts his right arm with her left hand, and takes one good swing at his armpit with her right hand. The cleaver cracks the bone only halfway through, so she repeats the movement until the arm is completely severed from his body, exposing skeletal bone and bloody pulpy flesh.

She proceeds to chop off the left arm, right leg, and then left leg until there is nothing but a sternal stump with a head attached. She wanted to clean his heart, so his soul would ascend to heaven. She grabs the cleaver and buries it right *smack* dab in the middle of his chest, cracking it open. She yanks out his heart and sets it on the oversized soap dish. Blood oozes from the valves and dribbles into the tub and down the drain. She's hopeful the soap residue will clean his dirty heart. The bones cracking and meat mashing unnerves her, so she leans over and turns on the shower radio.

Frank Sinatra. How fitting. Logan loved Sinatra. In her mind, this is a sign that she's doing the right thing and sending him off with a bang. Miranda smiles and resumes chopping, cutting, and bagging him up. His 6'2" height was cut down to size in a matter of a couple hours. Bag by bag, she lugs his limbs downstairs into the basement, then pushes them up and over into the freezer.

Once she is back in the bathroom, she lets out a sigh of relief. She is almost done. There's still some skin stragglers and veins in the tub and on the floor, as well as blood splotches resembling paint splatter. Miranda grabs a big jug of bleach and fills a bucket with water. There's a hand towel hanging around the shower head.

She finishes off her red plum juice and grabs a piece of fruit from the bowl on the kitchen table. She puts on her gloves and gets to work disinfecting the area and removing all traces of what happened earlier. Marvin Gaye is playing in the background.

N.M. Chaney

Papyrophiliac. Bibliophile. Horroraholic. Hopeless romantic. Spiritual. Work in progress. Thankful. Animal lover. I enjoy writing and reading short stories.

The Hollow Crown
Anniee Bee

Once Upon a Time . . .

There was a kingdom where the sun never rose. A place locked in twilight, where rivers ran black, and the wind carried the whispers of the dead. At the heart of this cursed land stood a hollow castle—its towers wrapped in thorned ivy, its throne forever empty.

The curse began with a queen's betrayal and a witch's vengeance. A single spell had trapped the land in an endless dusk, dooming every child born within it to bear the sins of their ancestors. But the worst fate belonged to the princess Seraphine, heir to the Hollow Crown.

She was born beneath an eclipse. Her skin was a deep, burnished bronze, glowing like embers in low candlelight. Her curls, thick and coiled like the twisting vines that choked the castle walls, held the scent of myrrh and rain. And her eyes, black as the void between stars, shifted watchfully.

Every night, she dreamed of voices calling her name. Of ghosts pressing their cold fingers against her throat. The kingdom whispered that she was not a girl, but a living omen.

They were right.

The Peasant's Secret

On the outskirts of the kingdom, in the dying light of the sunless world, lived a peasant boy named Elias. He had nothing—no family, no name worth speaking of—only a secret that could destroy everything.

He knew the truth of the curse.

The spell that doomed their kingdom had not come from an old witch's wrath but from the hands of royalty. The Queen, Seraphine's mother, had been the one to seal the fate of their land, having traded the souls of her people for eternal power. But the spell turned against her, leaving the throne empty and the princess haunted by ghosts not of her making.

Elias had spent his life searching for a way to end the curse before it consumed them all. And only one path remained.

Seraphine had to die.

The Truth Behind the Crown

On the eve of her seventeenth year, Seraphine stood before the shattered mirror in the castle's grand hall. The whispers had grown louder. The air was thick with restless spirits.

"Find the boy," they murmured in a language older than the kingdom itself. "He carries the knife meant for your heart."

And so she did.

She found Elias standing at the gates of the ruined cathedral, the ancient symbols of protection carved into his wrists like a warning. He wore a cloak of woven reeds, the same pattern worn by the last free people before the curse had fallen. A silver dagger gleamed in his hand, etched with markings from the old tongue.

"I have to do this," he said. "The only way to break the curse is with royal blood. Your blood."

Seraphine did not flinch. She had always known she was meant to die. The ghosts had told her as much. But now, standing before the boy who had searched for answers his whole life, she saw something they had not whispered—doubt.

"If I die," she asked, "will the curse truly break? Or will it only feed the darkness?"

The spirits howled. The dagger trembled in Elias's grip. And, in that moment, Seraphine saw the dark *truth:*

The curse had never been hers to bear. It had been Elias's all along.

His family had been the first to die in the queen's sacrifice. His bloodline had been tied to the spell. If he killed her, the cycle would only restart, trapping another soul, dooming another kingdom.

"I was never meant to die for this," she whispered. "But you were."

A Crown of Ashes

The wind howled as Seraphine took the dagger from Elias's hands.

Then, she drove the blade into his heart.

The moment Elias fell, the sky cracked open. For the first time in her life, she saw the light of the sun, golden and flickering, and bright like a candle in the dark. Light flooded the land, chasing away the ghosts, lifting the fog, and burning away the twisted remnants of the past.

The Kingdom was free.

Seraphine was not.

She turned back to the castle, where the empty throne awaited. The curse needed a soul to end. And though Elias was dead, the Hollow Crown still required a ruler.

As the kingdom rejoiced, Seraphine sat upon the throne, her hands stained with blood. The golden light dimmed—The Kingdom faded back into dusk.

The throne was filled, yet the Kingdom was cursed anew.

This time, there would be no escape.

Anniee Bee

Anniee Bee is an award-winning author and book reviewer with over thirty published books. She crafts bold and captivating stories across genres, delivering compelling narratives that resonate with readers.

The Girl Without a Face

J. V. Sadler

Here, here comes the girl without a face. Her features are nonexistent—smooth and pale where a nose, mouth, and eyes should be. When she goes into town, the people stare, and the children point their fingers at the sight of a girl with a flat slab of flesh where her face should be.

"Look at the *thing*," the bakery woman comments, uncaring that the girl can hear. "*It* is quite hideous."

"I agree," replies her husband, even louder. "Repelling and odd, indeed!"

"Doesn't she live in that termite-infested stump out in the woods?"

"Oh, that's just a rumour," her husband chuckles.

A basket swings at the girl's side with each step. Her grip is firm on the basket without crushing its delicate twig-woven handle. Inside it lies a piece of her heart, her true self, which she daydreams of unveiling. She travels to the dressmaker, hoping this will be the day she discovers herself.

The dressmaker asks, "Lace or linen?" His back is turned to the girl as he meddles with an impressive collection of fabric.

The girl does not—cannot—answer.

The dressmaker turns to speak again. "Lace or —" Upon seeing the faceless girl, the dressmaker drops his fabric. "You!" he exclaims. "You're the nameless girl. The unknown girl."

Some days, the faceless girl would peek into the dressmaker's window like a tiny mouse admiring a piece of cheddar. She had a feeling the man knew she had been watching him during his craftsmanship. She had a feeling the man would be the only person who could help her. Today, she gathered the courage to finally meet this dressmaker.

"Are you here for a dress?" he asks.

She shakes her head and points to a needle and thread at his workstation.

"You want to learn to sew? The young, dressmaking apprentice. Wouldn't that sound nice?"

The girl shakes her head once more, points to her lack of a face, then to the needle and thread again.

"Ah, I see . . ."

She nods furiously.

"I will, I will, but only for something in return. Do you have a gold coin? Anything of value?"

After digging in her basket, the girl presents the dressmaker a handmade leather-bound book just slightly bigger than his hand.

Without needing to flip through its pages, the dressmaker knows the book is of great quality. He could sell this at an exuberant price easily. "This'll do," he says. "Come back tonight when the farmer calls for his pig."

The faceless girl returns home (if one could call a hollowed-out fallen log a "home"). She has a chipper skip in her step that she had only once, and that was when she made friends with a wiggle-nose hare. The hare she never named loved to ruin the garden she had tried to grow outside the hollowed log. Knotweed and cinquefoil crept through. The girl felt quite accomplished with her horticulture. Then, she watched day by day as the wiggle-nose hare chomped through it all. She wept when she found the hare filled with buckshot. The creature's crude remains would go to hang from the butcher's hook, eventually for someone to purchase.

Here, here she is, skipping to her forest away from the village, past the abandoned brick cottage, and beyond the faded welcoming sign with the barely legible letters S N IR: It once read SUNMIRE. The farmer, her nearest neighbor, had painted the sign long ago. But that is all she knows about the quiet, staring man. The only sounds she ever hears from him are his pig calls and dog whistles. On the odd times they catch each other's glances, he stares into the endless paleness of her nonexistent face, and she pretends to know what it is like to wonder deeply into another's eyes.

The girl's knees *thud* to the ground. Her skirt, aided by green, damp moss, cushions the impact. She crawls into the decomposing log she calls home (yes, the rumors are correct) and sleeps.

***

"Sooey!"

The faceless girl scrambles awake.

"Soooooey!"

She hears the farmer call for his pig in a deafening high pitch and elongated high vowels. Nighttime had come. The girl gathers herself and hurries to the dressmaker.

A voice could echo on the streets of Sunmire this time of night. Villagers snub their candles and put their children to sleep. But this evening, one humble shop lantern remains on. The girl reaches her balled fist to knock on the door, but the dressmaker opens it before she can make a sound.

"Quiet," he whispers. "Come in. Come in."

The dressmaker is prepared for the faceless girl. Coverings on the windows for privacy. Dimness except for a lamp and a flickering candle on a long table in the middle of the shop. Thick and clean wool sheets protect the floor. Stacks of discolored, lye-stained rags and a bucket of water. Needle and thread.

Needle and thread . . . The girl could sing if it had not been for the absence of a mouth. Her heart bounces around in her chest, tickles her belly, and reaches the top of her throat, almost making her choke. Emotions of all kinds fill her tiny frame as she rushes to lie on the long table set just for her. Heavy, scratchy ropes slither over her waist and arms. Ropes also around her chin and forehead secure her head in place.

"So I can work without you squirming," the dressmaker says, tightening the restraints.

When the dressmaker knots the rope, the girl attempts to wiggle, half expecting the restraints to loosen—she cannot move an inch. She wishes she could inhale a puff of air, then exhale to slow her thumping chest. Rubbing against the restraints irritates her wrists. She submits. Unexpected fuzzy things brush both the girl's hands, and she instinctively grabs onto them.

"Something to squeeze. Bunny lovies I made," says the dressmaker.

Water sploshes as the man scrubs his hands. He sits at the table, then studies the girl's slab of a face. He is an artist; no measurements needed, he assures. The sewing needle glows bright red when he twirls it in the candle flame. Imagining the blaze discoloring the sharp metal, the girl digs her nails into the table. Maybe the pain of wood splintering underneath her nails can distract her, she pleads in her mind.

"Squeeze, love."

Her lungs expel air to the top of her trachea. She does have a larynx. Actually, besides lips, she has many parts that could operate together to form one good *AH*! Her vocal cords vibrate. The faceless girl's throat attempts all the usual mechanics of screaming as the dressmaker stitches her a new face. Not one sound surfaces. Not one cry or piercing howl.

The room is quiet aside from the girl's attempts at thrashing, the dressmaker's weight shifting, and a buzzing cicada that found its way into the shop.

It isn't until the dressmaker ties the last knot of the last stitch at the bottom left corner of the girl's stringed mouth that vocalization finally occurs. The no-longer-faceless girl lets out a long *yooowl* that surely alerts the sleeping villagers. Subsequent wild sounds flee from her new mouth. She cannot understand herself. She fumbles over her exploring tongue and chatters her unaccustomed teeth. The dressmaker hurries to undo the restraints.

"Show us who you are," he says to the no longer faceless girl.

Overwhelmed with gratitude, the girl embraces the dressmaker. She sees his face clearly: wrinkled forehead, chin pimples, nose hairs, and a developing unibrow. He looks beautiful. She sniffs him, too. A sweat-riddled shirt, natural bodily musk, and his hands covered in mess from the procedure.

He smells heavenly. She hears the chaos forming outside. It sounds like the world to her.

The no-longer-faceless girl bolts outside to see a crowd of villagers investigating the dressmaker's shop. Every villager appears magnificent, just like the dressmaker. Their buck teeth, patched-up clothes, callus bare feet poking through worn soles, matted hair, and midnight breath stench—all wonderful.

"You-you-your f-f-face." One villager points.

Another villager holds a bucket of water and a lamp to the girl's face. She stares into the water and sees . . . she sees . . . *Is this me?*

Someone finally asks, "What's your name, girl?"

***

SUNMIRE. The farmer had repainted the welcoming sign. Villagers stroll through town as usual, conversing with one another about how nice the day is. The dressmaker's shop is usually busy, but today he takes a moment to flip through a leather-bound book.

He couldn't bring himself to sell the book that the girl had given him. Twenty days after creating her new face, he visited her fallen log in an attempt to return it. But the girl was nowhere to be found. Two bunny lovies waited for him on the large log, leaning against one another like lovers watching a sunset together.

The dressmaker thought the book empty. And it is empty except for one sentence on the first page written neatly in a cursive that could've been mistaken for a royal's calligraphy:

I hereby name myself Photini

J.V. Sadler

J.V. Sadler is a writer and poet from Cincinnati, Ohio. Her work has been featured on NIGHTLIGHT: A Horror Fiction Podcast. Her first book Licking is a collection of macabre horror short stories. You can find all her socials and links at https://linktr.ee/JVSadler.

Whispers in the Wood
Ginny Davis

Sali flew quickly across the enormous forest. Her silver wings, which matched her hair, were worn and tired, but she couldn't stop. Her family was weak from worry, sickness, and starvation, yet she couldn't let her spirit and powers weaken. She had to get to an elder and knew just the one who could help. She hoped to find food and medicine for her brood along the way.

The tree nymph had gone out many times to forage for herbs and nutrients to keep her family alive. Every pass she made became increasingly dangerous than the last. She tried to stay out of sight while she soared toward something, anything that would help.

As Sali flew, memories flooded her mind of how they had lived in the thick dark woods for thousands of years. Before man. Then, alongside the native folk in harmonious peace.

It wasn't until the invaders came that things changed. Within the last eighty years, the vast, green forest had steadily been destroyed.

She was so lost in her thoughts, she supposed she had missed a turn. She found herself in an unfamiliar clearing. While trying to locate a familiar landmark, a large crash startled her. She spun around, darted across the clearing towards the noise. Once she made it to the other side, she hid in the trees.

There lying on the lush, forest floor was the elder she had been searching for: the oldest, magical tree known to the fairy folk. The surrounding family of trees were gone; only stumps remained. She fluttered closer to the elder, overcome by the lingering stench of humans who had recently been there and the toxic fumes of their equipment.

"Cocci, Cocci," she whispered. "Can you hear me?"

Cocci's eyes opened, weak mand sad. "Sali, they've taken us all. You must act quickly."

Sali listened closely, silver tears running down her muddy face.

Cocci motioned to the bottom of his trunk. "Go to the soil. There are nutrients. Plant what you find. Afterwards, your family should be able to prosper for hundreds of years. It's too late for me. I know you and your family are in desperate need. Do it quickly before my eyes close one last time."

Sali flew quickly to the base of the great old tree and collected four large pouches of the warm, glowing soil. She was about to return to Cocci, when she heard a strange rumbling. She turned and saw an empty spot she knew well; it was gray now with a terrible stench coming from it. It seemed to pulse, making the putrid smell stronger.

"Poor Alnus," she whispered. This was Cocci's mate, a tree that was older than the wood itself. She held back tears as she flew back to face Cocci.

"They've left me to be torn apart. They unleashed a darkness by cutting down Alnus. Be gone by the time they get back. Don't take this darkness back to your family. Do not get any of it on you." Cocci closed his eyes and stirred no more.

Sali stayed with Cocci. Early the next morning when the invaders returned, she hid at the edge of the clearing, using a large stump as cover. The men moved in with their trucks and equipment. They prepared to butcher Cocci. They were halfway to her when they all became stuck fast in the rancid muck. Suddenly, the earth in which they were stuck swallowed them slowly. The men fought to get free but soon tired themselves out. They screamed but no one could hear them. Much like they didn't hear the screams of the great trees that they destroyed.

Sali watched with a mixture of sadness and satisfaction as the decaying earth digested the men. Some of the men tried to reach their arms out of the rotted muddy lagoon. She looked at Alnus one last time, secured her pouches, and traveled back home.

She didn't notice that the men's arms reaching out for safety had transformed into branches overnight. When the company responsible for cutting down the trees came searching for the men, they were shocked at what they found. They tried to rush in and recover the bodies and equipment. The first truck got stuck and sank, but the driver was able to climb out of the roof to get away. No one could get close enough to retrieve anything from the pit.

Over decades, the men became what they had sought to destroy. The trees were special; they were dank and smelled as if they had spoiled. Their wood was no good but held on tightly to the earth. This assembly of trees spread quickly through the clearing, making it impossible for anyone to get to healthy woods.

Sali would come back and visit from time to time, but the souls of elders taken too soon haunted this part of the forest And these souls were angry, stirring restlessly, waiting for the return of the invaders.

Ginny Davis

Hi! I'm Ginny Davis- Author, Writer and Novelist. Writing is my passion and writing dark thriller tales are my love. That and a splash of magic make for an amazing ride into the unknown. Close your eyes and buckle up.

RAVEN
Miracle Austin

Mama was always telling Carter to be mindful of the paths she chose. She especially warned her about the crooked roads being gateways to supernatural creatures, unexplained beings, and hidden, haunted objects waiting to climb out of their dark graves and travel into our world.

Little did Carter know that an unexpected encounter was ahead of her tonight on the way to the annual Kappa Alpha Kappa Golden Formal with her friends . . .

Carter and Bonnie pledged together during their freshman year at Buella University and became good friends. They roomed together at their sorority house and decided to purchase the same formal dress ensemble.

"Carter, hurry up! The boys will be here any minute," Bonnie rattled off as she balanced glittery, golden feathers in her thick, curly hair in the standup mirror near the bedroom door.

"I'm almost ready. I just need to find my gold pumps with the red rhinestone bows on the back. Have you seen them?" Carter asked, departing their oversized closet while placing the metal backs on her five-carat, heart-shaped ruby earrings.

"Oh, I didn't think you were going to wear them tonight," Bonnie replied, clicking Carter's Louboutin heels like she was filming that scene in *The Wizard of Oz*.

"Hand them over, thief!" Carter demanded with both hands on her shimmering, golden hips.

"Come on, you know my legs look better in them than yours," Bonnie chuckled with a twirl. "Even though they're already burning the sides of my pinky toes." She lifted one foot up at a time and balanced herself against the bedpost to massage them with her hands.

"*They* don't want you in them," Carter snapped.

A loud car horn sounded off. Their dates, Harry and Shannon, were waiting in a pearl Suburban. Bonnie trotted to the front door, opened it, and yelled out, "Give us five minutes!" as she held up the palm of her hand.

Shannon waved back at Bonnie and turned up the music as he blew smoke out from his e-cigarette and leaned further back in his seat; coconut and mango scented puff clouds floated inside the car.

Bonnie closed the door and said, "It's time to go." She grabbed her fringe, champagne shawl and purse.

"Umm, aren't you forgetting something?" Carter interrogated her while rolling her eyes.

"I don't think so. Everything: head, body, and outfit—all bangin' and gorgeous—check, check, and check. I'm all good and ready," Bonnie said, winking at Carter.

Carter stared her down–pointing at the shoes and tapping her black-stockinged foot on the carpet floor. "The shoes, Bonnie."

Bonnie kicked them off her feet and huffed. She pounded her feet on the floor and beelined straight to the closet, flicked the light on, and tore boxes from the shelves.

Carter slipped her shoes on and grabbed her belongings. Bonnie marched out and shouted, "You know, I'm glad I'm not wearing your last season shoes. These are cuter, anyhow."

"Guess what, Einstein. Those are mine, too." Carter whispered, stepping out of their sorority house. They were the last ones to leave. Their sorority mom waved and locked up behind them.

Bonnie jerked the passenger door open, flopped into the leather, heated seat, and slammed the door. Carter slipped in the back and shut the door quietly. Shannon jumped up and looked at Bonnie and then back at Carter.

"You two must've had another girl fight," he said and laughed under his breath. "Right, Harry?"

Bonnie remained silent and sniffed the air. "Shannon, you told me that you were quitting."

"I can't go one night without you nagging me about that. Just shut up and enjoy the drive," he commanded in a thundering tone, pointing his finger in her face.

Bonnie squirmed in her seat.

Shannon blew smoke in her face, placed the car in gear to drive, and sped off Buella University's campus.

Their small town of Buella, Louisiana was a little over an hour from New Orleans. The Kappa Alpha Kappa Golden Formal hosted over ten thousand guests. They celebrated together once a year at a fancy, hotel resort. Money, music, a celebrity speaker, award ceremony, and exotic foods from Caribbean and African countries were all part of the magical night.

Carter buckled her seatbelt and mouthed to Harry, "Aren't you going to say something to him?"

"About what?" Harry mumbled. "That's my boy's girl and their business. Not mine or yours. Look, it's starting to snow. Come on over closer to me." He popped a mint in his mouth and moistened his lips.

Raising her eyebrows, Carter replied, "I'm good where I'm at. I don't want to mess up my make-up or wrinkle my dress for our group photo later tonight."

"Yeah, I guess you got a point," Harry said and started scrolling on his phone.

Carter attempted to grab Bonnie's attention by texting her, but Bonnie reframed from corresponding back. Carter frowned, adjusted her seatbelt, and watched the snow fall from her window. It hadn't snowed in Buella since 2007.

The snow had covered the roads. The gas light on the car's dash started blinking. Shannon ignored it. "Um, don't you think it's time to fill up," Carter suggested.

"I know when I need to gas up. Harry, handle your girl, man. Remember what we talked about," Shannon barked, sounding like a Rottweiler.

"Excuse me, handle your girl!" Carter shouted and dug her heels into the floor. "First of all, I'm a young lady, and I'm no one's girl."

Bonnie turned around quickly to face Carter, holding her index finger against her lips. She whispered, "Please, Carter . . ." A solo tear ran down her cheek. "Don't get him more upset."

Carter breathed a long sigh. Bonnie resumed her position in the front seat. Shannon continued driving. Harry looked into Carter's eyes, before she turned back towards her window. A mileage sign read fifty more miles to New Orleans.

The car started slowing down. Shannon exited off the highway as soon as he could. They coasted on a curvy, back road. They were led to a small gas station.

No cars were parked in the front, but a few were in the back. Colorful lights decorated the side of the building. Hundreds of ravens were perched on top of the building and on the lampposts. They filled the swaying, loblolly pine trees.

Shannon found an empty gas pump with ease. Harry remained with him while he finished pumping gas. Carter and Bonnie made their way inside the store to find a restroom to freshen up, carefully tiptoeing to avoid slipping on the icy pavement. Harry and Shannon browsed the store for their favorite snacks and drinks.

As Shannon was scooping up some lollipops in his hand and unwrapping one to pop inside of his mouth, he started salivating at what he saw in front of him. Harry was kneeling down and flipping through a car magazine. Shannon pulled him up by his shoulders. "Three o'clock . . ." he whispered.

A tall and slender lady with ebony hair and tangerine highlights stood on a ladder organizing merchandise on the shelves. Her hair was rolled up in a thick bun with dangling ringlets swinging back and forth on the sides of her face. A low-cut dark, mini denim dress outlined her voluptuous figure. If she moved the wrong way, then the seams of the dress might have busted wide open.

Shannon almost swallowed the candy and the white stick. He couldn't keep his eyes off her. He shoved Harry out of the way with his legs and slid sideways on the smooth floor towards the counter as if riding a skateboard, but stopped at the base of the counter before scratching his golden Santoni Derby shoes.

He rested his arms on the counter and said in his best Barry White voice, "You're the most beautiful woman I've ever seen. You have to tell me your name and give me your number."

The lady smiled, scanned the room with her eyes, and stepped off the ladder to face her newest admirer. "Why are you flirting with me in front of your girlfriend?"

Shannon stood up and flung his body around in his custom-made black Brioni velvet tuxedo with tails. "Girl-what?" he asked, turning on the balls of his feet to face her.

"The one who flew into the ladies room almost ten minutes ago to unleash a bucket of tears," the lady pointed out.

Pulling the lollipop out of his mouth slowly, he paused. "Oh, she's not my girlfriend . . . just my date for a few hours. I'm not that guy—you know, the committing type. However, you could change my whole philosophy tonight, if you give me your number. I just may consider becoming monogamous with you." He winked at her, removing his cell from his inner jacket pocket.

"Where are y'all headed tonight, all dressed up like y'all are about to receive Oscars?" She slid back onto the step ladder.

His eyes were locked on her long legs. "An annual frat formal in New Orleans," he replied with a slight stutter.

Adjusting a hairpin in her hair. "It must be a fancy one."

Harry bumped into Shannon's side and mumbled into his ear, "You're right about her . . ." He clicked his tongue.

Carter and Bonnie came up behind him. Carter tapped Harry on the shoulder, placing some snacks on the counter. "What were you saying, Harry?"

"Nothing. Right, Shannon?" he replied, taking in an extended gulp and running his hands through his tight curls.

Shannon blew out a loud sigh. "Right, nothing, especially now."

Bonnie hugged his arm.

The lady stood up and rang them up for everything. Shannon found a marker on the counter and jotted his number on the back of a hundred-dollar bill. "Keep the change." He pushed it towards her, tapping the money with his hand. Bonnie jerked it away from him and flipped it over.

"Wow, really, Shannon? Right in front of me? Unbelievable! My sisters tried to warn me about you." Bonnie sprinted towards the door.

"Shannon, of all nights, why? Why? Just take us home! The night is only going to get worse," Carter yelled out.

"We're going to the frat celebration. If y'all want to stay in the hotel room all night, then be my guest." He shrugged his shoulders and focused his attention back on the lady. "I'm sure that I won't have a problem finding a replacement." He stared at the lady.

Carter looked him up and down. "Harry, are you coming?"

"Yeah, I'll be right behind you in a bit," Harry replied with his head down.

Carter left the items on the counter, bolted away, and jerked the door open to find Bonnie.

"Take the money," Shannon demanded. "Keep the change and my number."

"No thanks. I'm good. It's on the house," the lady insisted. She placed the snacks inside a plastic bag and pushed it in Shannon's direction.

Shannon pulled a cold drink from the sack, twisted the bottle cap off, tilted the bottle to his open mouth, and took a huge swig.

A little girl, possibly eight or nine years old, with loose, rainbow ribbons weaved through her braided ponytails ran out from the back and hugged the lady around her waist. She turned around to wave at Shannon and Harry.

Stumbling back a step or two, Shannon spat out his drink, which splashed mostly on the counter, but some landed on the back of the girl's shirt. He fired out, "Dang, what the hell is that? She's uglier than sin!" He laughed. "She's the creepiest thing I've ever seen. When she was born, someone should've found a swamp and thrown her in with a few hungry gators to end her misery."

Harry placed his hands over his mouth to quiet his laughter.

The little girl's forehead was extended several inches longer than normal. Her entire face appeared to have tough, armored scales similar to an alligator. She was nearly toothless with webbed hands and pointy ears. The lady grabbed a towel from underneath the counter and patted her back with it.

Bending down to wipe the girl's tears away from her face, the lady hugged her and escorted her to the back room. Upon her return, the stomping of her heels made the floor vibrate.

"Did you feel that, Shannon?" Harry asked, grabbing the edge of the counter after slightly losing his balance.

"Yeah, I never heard of earthquakes around here," Shannon said.

The lady marched over to him.

"Have you any idea what you've done?" she asked.

Shannon looked at Harry. "Nope." He peeled the wrapper off a candy bar and stuffed it in his mouth.

"She was born that way," the lady replied with a Southern, sharp drawl.

"Oh, snap. That thing is yours?" Shannon asked, almost choking and coughing. He picked up his bag. "Man, you gotta wake up to that thing every morning. Dress and feed it. I would lose my mind. I feel sorry for you."

Harry glanced down at his watch. "We need to get back on the road—let's get out of here, man."

Shannon headed towards the door behind Harry.

Before Harry pushed the glass door open and the bell above his head could jangle, the lady shouted out, "No! I feel sorry for *you*, tonight."

Shannon frowned and rolled his eyes. "Whatever . . . I don't associate with freaks so lose my number." He glided his hand over his muscular chest. He flung the driver's door open and jumped in the driver's seat. Harry slid in the passenger seat.

Bonnie was sobbing on Carter's lap and sniffling with a tissue clutched in her hand. Carter was stroking her hair with a firm scowl towards Shannon and Harry.

Shannon turned around to face them. "Bonnie, you got less than an hour to clean yourself up. I have a reputation to uphold."

He pushed the ignition button and touched the GPS option on the screen. The GPS read out loud in a Jamaican accent as Shannon drove: *Delays ahead, due to a car pileup on I-10. Alternate route now calculating . . . please take Deadrift Country Road for twenty-seven miles.*

When Shannon turned on Deadrift, there were no other cars on the road. Despite the accumulating snow, Shannon drove over a hundred miles an hour. He turned the music up loud. An instrumental track by Evanescence echoed all around the car. Snow pelted down. Shannon flipped on the windshield wipers.

"You shouldn't treat Bonnie like you do, and you really need to slow down!" Carter announced, reaching up to slap the back of his headrest.

"This is my car, and I'll drive how I want. Don't touch my car again, ever! Just keep your opinions to yourself. I can do whatever I want. Relax and be glad you're not my date tonight," he hissed, staring at her in his rearview mirror with penetrating, serial killer-like dark eyes.

Bonnie squeezed Carter's hand hard and mumbled, "I'm not attending the dance with him tonight or any other night. I'm done."

"Good! I've been wondering when you make this decision for you. We can catch a ride back to campus with Evelyn and Josh. I know she won't mind at all."

"Thank you for being a supportive friend to me, Carter."

"You know I love you and would do anything for you."

They embraced.

"Now, you should really put your seatbelt on," Carter recommended, wiping Bonnie's face with a tissue.

Before Bonnie could secure herself in her seat, Shannon hit a patch of ice. The car swerved and spun several times.

Shannon slammed on his breaks. Bonnie's body flung between the seats. Carter tried to grab her arms, but the vehicle hit a large, unknown object in the road causing it to fly up in the air. It landed on its side and slid halfway down the road.

Carter opened her eyes. She felt something wet running down the side of her forehead. She reached up and discovered it was blood. Her head was throbbing. She looked all around. She noticed Bonnie, Harry, and Shannon had all been thrown out of the car in different directions.

All of the windows were shattered. Carter slid her heel off and used its sharp tip to cut two strips off her ruined dress. She dabbed as much of the blood away as she could with the first strip. She tied the other strip around her forehead. She slipped her pump back on her foot.

She fumbled with her seatbelt for over two minutes, until she finally heard it click open. She pulled the strap from around her and crawled out the side window. Shards of glass pierced her hands and arms; she ripped additional strips from her dress to wrap them. She checked on Bonnie first. Blood saturated the snow under her body.

Kneeling over Bonnie, Carter felt for her pulse—she didn't have one. Then, she pressed her hands down on her friend's chest. No heartbeat. She saw a long tree branch protruding through her side. Tears filled her eyes. She thought back when her and Bonnie first met. Bonnie didn't like Carter at first, but after Carter helped her survive sorority pledge week they became inseparable.

Carter inspected Bonnie's still face for a few minutes for any signs of life. With no reason to hesitate, she slid her hand down to close Bonnie's eyes.

A loud cough came from behind her. The snow had slowed down.

"Help me!"

She attempted to stand up, but dropped back down to the wet ground.

"Carter, I'm hurt. Help me!" Shannon moaned out like an injured animal. He screamed out, "Something stabbed my leg! I can't move or feel my legs."

"You deserve to suffer. If you'd just slowed down when I begged you to or just took us back home, then Bonnie would still be here . . . with me. I would still have my friend. You never deserved her." Tears rolled down Carter's cheeks.

She searched the area and found Harry's body resting against a tree on the opposite of where she was. She made her way to where he was. "Harry, Harry!" Carter screamed out.

He didn't respond.

"Stop wasting your time. I'm sure he's dead by now," Shannon said.

"Help me. I'm still alive," Shannon wailed. "I can see what's in my leg now. This can't be possible."

Carter turned around and stopped. "What?"

"A three-foot huge black feather impaled my freakin' leg. It won't budge!" he whined.

She ambulated back towards him.

Winds picked up and pushed everything—the living and cold bodies, the vehicle, and debris back. Something landed in the middle of them with feathered, black silky wings that nearly touched the ground. Goosebumps covered Carter's arms. The creature turned around to face Shannon—its long hair blew above its slender waist.

"Well, I see you followed your GPS directions after that nasty, highway wreck," she announced. Her wings fluttered up and down.

"Who are you?" Shannon gasped with quivering lips.

Carter shivered and wrapped her arms around her chest to try to stay warm.

"You were begging me earlier for my name. I guess it's time for me to share," she said with a boastful laugh. Her eyes were an icy blue and seemed to glow.

"Wait, you're the lady from the store back there," he motioned with his nearly paralyzed arms.

"Give this boy a prize!" she popped off. "My name is Adina. I'm here to take care of you and your other friend over there." Her elongated wing pointed in Carter's direction.

"What are you?" Carter asked in a shaky tone.

"Something you don't ever want to cross or piss off, but some just can't help themselves, sweet Carter. I need to take care of my primary target, right over there, first. Shannon is your name, correct?"

"Now, wait a minute. I didn't do anything to you," Shannon snarled. His hands were freezing, blue, and throbbing.

"That's right, but you caused my daughter unnecessary trauma. Plus, you're truly a despicable person from the moment I smelled you before you entered my store. I know all about boys like you. You don't deserve to exist," Adina declared, stroking her feathers with one of her hands.

Carter watched, shivering with her hands deep inside of her dress pockets.

Adina's piercing eyes landed on Carter.

"What are you?" Shannon shouted from his trembling lips while clutching his side. "I'm not afraid of you."

"You will be," Adina sneered.

"Listen, if you help me, my parents will make a generous donation to your little monster's charity," Shannon boasted and spat saliva mixed with blood towards Adina's feet.

Adina plucked out five of her feathers from her wings. They instantly grew back. She then threw them like darts around his neck. They pierced his jugular vein—blood flowed out rapidly. Shannon let out loud cries for a brief moment until his entire body froze. Within ten seconds, his body crumbled into the snow.

Adina leapt into the air, shrieking, "You should never cause harm of any kind to a mama's child—she might just come after you in a way you never *imagined*."

Hovering above Carter, she lifted up her pointy, plum and silver nails with jagged, onyx tips. They raked through Carter's icy hair. She dragged her index finger down her cold jawline, lowered herself to the ground, and kneeled to meet Carter's eyes.

"You and your friends are all guilty by association. I'm sorry I have to end your life as well—you're merely a causality and most of all a *witness,* which is a big no-no for my kind. You seemed to be so sweet, confident, and an advocate for your late sorority sister. I wished you would've gone out like her or your boyfriend from the ice patch I created," Adina explained.

"You initiated the havoc on the highway to steer us here . . ." Carter realized.

"Yes, you pick up quick."

"You don't have to do this?" Carter sniffled. "I promise I won't tell anyone what happened here tonight."

"Awe . . . I just can't take that risk. I must do what's always been done. Don't take it personally."

Carter attempted to scoot away from her, but Carter's red, rhinestone bows on her golden shoes slipped against a rock and cast a fiery spark high in the air.

Adina noticed and examined. "Oh . . . those are a find. I must have them. You won't be needing them anymore once I eliminate you." Her hands reached out to touch them. A spark shot out from them, burning one side of Adina's face, tossing her into the air, and flinging her against a tree several feet away from Carter.

A purplish light covered Carter's body. The ice melted from her hair and her clothing. She was no longer shaking.

Adina flew back over to Carter. "Who **gifted** you those magical beauties on your feet?" she asked with trembling eyes focused on Carter.

"You're nervous, aren't you?" Carter smirked.

"I need to know," Adina begged. "Those shoes possess a dual spell—*healing* and *protection*." She stared at Carter. "I've been searching for years for something like that to transform my daughter. Tell me!"

Carter noticed the wounds on her hands and face healing. She stood up without a limp or stumble. The purple glow continued to shine over her. She went over to the truck and searched for her purse. She found her phone and called 911. "Adina, my mama gave them to me for my nineteenth birthday."

"Who's your mama?" Adina asked in a panicked voice. Some of her feathers started spiraling off to the ground and igniting into temporary flames. Adina's eyes widened three times her normal size.

"Nyra . . . *Nyra Laveau*. She told me to always be careful of ravens, but I never understood until tonight. Y'all have a nasty taste for revenge, regardless if some are actually inno-cent. You ravens need do a better job before you *mark* each person in a group," Carter cackled.

"Let me reverse everything," Adina begged as more fiery feathers melted and swarmed like a tornadic thunderstorm around her body.

"I know and you know that you're lying. I'll make sure to share my entire experience with the Laveau Council. You killed my friend, and I'll never forget that. You probably want to start making living arrangements for your little one sooner rather than later, Adina," Carter stated calmly.

"Please, please . . . let me make it up to you."

"Stop begging. I guess that I can ask the council to grant you mercy–I can't make any promises that they will. Afterall, you took care of Shannon. I'd plans to dispose of him myself before the end of the night—he's been way overdue."

Smoky, iridescent flames encircled and danced around Carter, melting the snow path as she strolled away from the crooked road. She halted. Clicked her heels three times and vanished into the deep, night abyss.

Miracle Austin

Miracle Austin is a Texan Gal who works in the medical social work arena by day and in the writer's world at night and weekends YA/NA author. She loves horror, Marvel/DC, Wednesday, Stranger Things, Goosebumps, 80s music, sparkles, and daydreaming up what to write next.

Miracle Austin

The Whispering Well
Tessa Lee-Thomas

Once upon a time, in the bustling borough of Brooklyn, there lived a girl named Ginger. She called a quaint brownstone in Bed-Stuy her home, a neighborhood teeming with life, where the hum of laughter and music filled the air during the day, but shadows grew long with whispered fears at night. The streets were alive with contradictions—a place where culture thrived, but danger lingered in the corners. Despite this, Ginger had an uncanny ability to see the beauty in the brokenness, the resilience in the people, and the hope in a world others deemed lost.

Among the locals, she was affectionately known as the *Princess of Bed-Stuy*. It wasn't a title she sought, but one bestowed upon her by a community that admired her heart. Ginger was always the first to lend a helping hand—the one assisting in organizing block parties to bring people together, the one who made sure children had a safe place to play. She had a rare gift for seeing people as they were and loving them anyway, a spark of warmth in a neighborhood where life could sometimes feel cold.

But to Ginger, the title felt like a weight she hadn't asked to bear. It was a reminder of the fractured world she so desperately wanted to mend. The high crime rates, the gang violence, the unspoken tensions . . . they loomed over her like a storm cloud, and she could feel the pressure to bring sunshine. She didn't want to be a princess; she wanted to be a catalyst for peace and joy. To her, the name was not a crown, but a burden, a constant whisper of the work left undone. Ginger longed for a world where she didn't need to fight so hard for unity, where the laughter of children didn't compete with sirens in the background, and where the people she loved could walk without fear.

Even so, Ginger didn't let the weight of her title crush her spirit. She continued to pour herself into her community, driven not by recognition but by the simple belief that change was possible. Her dream wasn't grand or gilded—it was simple and profound: a life filled with peace, where everyone could feel safe, seen, and celebrated.

Ginger had been raised by a single mother, a woman whose strength and resilience had been the foundation of their lives. Her mother, a fierce and brilliant lawyer at a prestigious law firm, had dedicated years to building a career that not only broke barriers but also ensured Ginger had a stable and loving home. Their brownstone, a legacy gifted by Ginger's great-grandparents, stood as a testament to generations of hard work and determination. It was more than just a house; it was a symbol of their family's perseverance and sacrifice.

But everything changed in an instant. A car running a red light struck Ginger's mother on her way home after a long day at work. The accident was devastating. The injuries were severe, leaving her unable to walk and confined to a wheelchair. The vibrant, independent woman who had been Ginger's guiding light was suddenly thrust into a life of dependency, her days filled with physical therapy sessions, doctor's visits, and the constant frustration of being unable to do the things she once took for granted.

The financial security her mother had worked so hard to build was a blessing, allowing them to maintain a modest but stable lifestyle despite the challenges. Yet, it was clear that money couldn't fix everything. Their lives had been irrevocably altered. Ginger's mother, once the embodiment of strength and self-reliance, was forced to rely on others for even the simplest tasks. It was a harsh reality, one that weighed heavily on both of them.

The accident happened just days before Ginger's sixteenth birthday. The gravity of their new situation overshadowed what should have been a milestone filled with celebration. While her mother insisted they would be fine and urged Ginger to focus on her education, Ginger couldn't ignore the weight of their circumstances. She felt an overwhelming responsibility to step up and help in any way she could.

Determined to lighten the burden, Ginger found a part-time job at a local bookstore. She worked evenings after school, carefully balancing her studies with her new respon-sibilities. The small paycheck she earned wasn't much, but every dollar felt like a contribution toward preserving the life her mother had built for them. The bookstore became more than just a place of work for Ginger—it was a sanctuary where she could find solace among the stories and charac-ters that filled its shelves, a quiet escape from the challenges waiting for her at home.

Though the accident had changed everything, Ginger's love and admiration for her mother only grew. Her moth-er's unyielding determination to adapt to her new reality inspired Ginger to face her own struggles with courage. To-gether, they navigated their changed world, leaning on each other in ways they never had before. The bond between them, forged in love and strengthened by adversity, became the anchor that kept them moving forward, even in the face of overwhelming challenges.

Now, at the age of 20, Ginger balanced her days immersed in her social work studies at Hunter College and her nights waiting tables at a small, dimly lit diner. Her studies were not merely academic pursuits; they were a mission. Growing up, Ginger had seen firsthand how systemic injustices shaped her community. Families struggling to make ends meet, children falling through the cracks of an overwhelmed system, and neighbors whose dreams were stifled by the weight of inequality—these were the realities of Bed-Stuy, and Ginger carried them in her heart.

Despite the challenges, Ginger's upbringing had instilled in her a profound sense of purpose. Privilege had occasionally brushed her life, like the time her mother's former employer had paid off lingering medical bills as a gesture of goodwill. But Ginger refused to let moments of fortune make her complacent. Instead, they deepened her resolve to uplift those who weren't as lucky. To her, every step forward was not just for herself but for her community.

When life allowed, Ginger sought refuge in nature. The bustling streets of Brooklyn, with their cacophony of car horns, chatter, and the ever-present rhythm of life, could feel suffocating. On those rare days off, she'd board a train heading upstate, longing for the serenity that only the forest could provide. The scent of pine, the rustle of leaves, and the soft crunch of earth beneath her boots offered her a peace she couldn't find anywhere else. It was her way of recharging, a brief escape from the relentless pace of city life. It was on one such journey, on a sunlit autumn afternoon, that Ginger's life changed forever.

***

The air was crisp, carrying with it the faint scent of fallen leaves. Ginger had ventured into the Sundown Wild Forest, a sprawling expanse known for its towering trees and labyrinthine trails. The forest that day was unusually quiet, as if holding its breath, and Ginger felt an inexplicable pull, a magnetic force that seemed to guide her steps off the well-trodden path. Though she hesitated, curiosity and an unshakable sense of destiny propelled her forward, deeper into the forest's mysterious heart.

The path was unlike the others, the ground barren and devoid of the vibrant greenery she had come to associate with the forest. Each step she took seemed to dampen the ambient sounds of nature, until an eerie stillness consumed the forest that surrounded her. Her steps faltered as she entered a grove of twisted trees, their gnarled branches reaching like skeletal hands. The bark of the trees was dark and cracked, oozing a viscous sap that glimmered faintly in the dim light. The air grew heavy, thick with an inexplicable sense of foreboding, and her breathing became shallow as though the atmosphere itself resisted her presence.

At the grove's center stood an ancient well, cloaked in thick vines that pulsed faintly, as though alive. The stones of the well were weathered and cracked, etched with symbols that seemed to shift and writhe when she tried to focus on them. The unnatural greenish-black glow emanating from the well cast long, distorted shadows across the grove, making the scene feel like something out of a nightmare. A faint humming sound, low and rhythmic, filled the air, vibrating through her chest and making her skin crawl.

"Ginger," a voice called, soft but insistent, as if it had arisen from the depths of her own mind.

Her heart thundered in her chest, the sound almost deafening in the oppressive silence. Yet curiosity, as sharp as it was dangerous, overpowered fear. She felt her feet moving, carrying her closer to the well. The cold, damp air clung to her skin as she peered over the edge. The water shimmered unnaturally, reflecting no light from above, only its own eerie luminescence. The depths seemed infinite, an abyss that threatened to swallow her whole.

Then the voice came again, low and velvety, dripping with menace. "Princess of Bed-Stuy, at last."

A chill raced down her spine, the fine hairs on her arms standing on end. She scanned the grove, her eyes darting to every shadow, but there was no one in sight. "Who's there?" she demanded, her voice wavering, barely above a whisper.

The water churned violently, its surface writhing as though something below struggled to break free. A face emerged, pale and otherworldly, its features both mesmerizing and grotesque. Hollow eyes that glowed like embers locked onto hers, and its lips curled into a smile that was anything but kind. The face was neither fully human nor fully monstrous, as though it existed on the border of both worlds.

"We've watched you," it said, its voice resonating in the stillness. The words carried a weight, as if they were not meant to be heard by mortal ears. "Your heart beats for the broken. You long to change their fates, to end their suffering. We can give you what you desire."

Ginger's breath caught in her throat. The face in the water seemed to grow larger, its eyes boring into hers as if searching her very soul. The air around her seemed to constrict, pressing down on her chest.

"What is it that my heart desires?" Ginger asked under her breath, the words escaping her lips before she could stop them.

The face's smile widened, revealing jagged teeth that gleamed unnaturally in the greenish light. "You seek justice," it said, its tone both knowing and mocking. "You seek to mend the fractures of your world, to lift the weight of despair from the shoulders of those who cannot bear it. Your heart desires to heal what is broken. Is this not so?"

Ginger's lips parted, but no words came. She could not deny the truth in its statement, but the malice in its tone made her stomach churn. She felt exposed, as though this creature could see every hidden part of her, even the parts she herself did not fully understand.

"You long for power," it continued, the water around its face rippling with each word. "The power to bend the world to your will, to banish hunger, despair, and pain. We can give it to you. All of it."

Her pulse quickened. The promises wrapped around her like a silken thread, enticing and suffocating all at once. The possibilities it offered flashed through her mind: children laughing instead of crying, families reunited, her mother's body healed. But deep within her, a warning bell rang, faint but persistent.

"At what cost?" she whispered, her voice trembling.

The entity chuckled, a sound like dry leaves scraping against stone. "Only what you do not need," it said. "Your light, your warmth, the spark that draws others to you. It is a small price, Princess of Bed-Stuy, for the power to change the world. Give it to us, and in return, you shall wield the power to bend the world to your will. No hunger. No despair. No pain."

The words enticed her like a vice. She thought of the children in her community, their hollow eyes and forced smiles. She thought of the families broken by poverty, the voices silenced by hardship. The well offered a chance to fix it all. But her instincts screamed at her to run.

"I need time," she said, stepping back.

The face twisted into a sneer. "Time is fleeting, child. And those who hesitate often lose more than they realize."

Ginger fled, the forest seeming darker and more oppressive with each step. Even as she boarded the train back to Brooklyn, the weight of the well's offer pressed on her chest. In the days that followed, Ginger couldn't escape the whispers. They haunted her dreams and followed her into waking life, a constant hum at the edge of her perception. Worse, her community seemed to spiral further into despair.

***

Families that had been barely surviving only weeks ago were now unraveling at an alarming pace. Their lives were crumbling into chaos. It was as if an unseen force had swept through, destroying everything in its path. People who once greeted Ginger warmly now avoided her gaze entirely, their once-bright smiles replaced by weary, shadowed expressions. They carried burdens they couldn't speak of, and their silence was deafening. It wasn't just their suffering that haunted her. She tried so hard to resist that suffocating feeling the darkness summoned as if retaliating, tightening its grip on her world. It was punishing her for her indecision, for hesitating when she should have acted, for daring to think she could save herself without saving them first.

The weight of her community's suffering pressed down on her, relentless and unyielding. Every look of despair, every broken smile, was a dagger to her heart. She couldn't take it anymore. The guilt, the pain, the overwhelming sense of failure—it all drove her to the edge. She knew what she had to do. With trembling hands and a heart filled with dread, she found herself walking back to the forest, back to the well.

This time, the forest pulsed with an eerie vitality. It wasn't silent as it had been before. Low groans echoed through the trees, rustling leaves whispered secrets she couldn't understand, and the faint crunch of footsteps trailed her every move. Though no one was there. The well stood waiting, its glow no longer faint but blinding, an unnatural, sickly green light that spilled out into the clearing, painting the trees with an unholy radiance.

"You've come back," the voice greeted her, smooth and triumphant, dripping with dark satisfaction.

Ginger swallowed hard, her throat dry and her chest heavy with the weight of her decision. "I am suffering," she said, her voice breaking. "But I can't bear to watch them suffer anymore." She paused, her breath shaky as she searched for strength. "But I need to know—what happens to me if I do this?"

The glow of the well intensified, and the voice shifted, its tone deeper and more menacing. A face emerged from the light—no longer human, but a monstrous distortion. Its elongated features and grotesque grin sent shivers down her spine. "You will become one of us," it said, its words deliberate and cold. "A guardian. A force of change. But you will walk this world alone, feared and unloved. Your sacrifice will go unnoticed by those you save, for they will never understand the cost."

Her hands trembled, and tears blurred her vision. She thought of the families, the children, the friends she had lost to the creeping darkness. She thought of how her own pain had grown unbearable, amplified by the pain of others, as if their suffering flowed through her veins. Her empathy had become a curse, a relentless agony that clawed at her from within.

Her lips quivered as she whispered, "If it means they'll have a chance, then take it." Her voice was resolute now, steadied by the fierce determination burning in her chest.

The well responded with a deep, rumbling laughter that reverberated through the clearing. "So be it," the voice hissed, triumphant. The light consumed her, and for a moment, there was nothing but searing pain and blinding brightness. When it faded, she stood transformed, a figure no longer tethered to the life she had known. She had become what the well promised—a guardian, a force of change. Alone, unloved, but resolute.

And though the forest fell silent once more, she could feel the weight of the world shift. Somewhere, the darkness began to retreat, and with it, a faint hope stirred in the lives of those she had sacrificed herself to save.

"You were always ours."

Ginger returned to Brooklyn that night, her heart aching with the knowledge of what she had given up.

Her powers were immense, terrifying in their magnitude. With a thought, she could ease suffering or amplify joy. Her community began to thrive, but Ginger was no longer a part of it. The people she once called friends now avoided her entirely, their eyes darting away as if looking at her was too much to bear. She had become a stranger to them, a shadow among the living.

The whispers never stopped. They lived inside her now, a chorus of voices feeding on her loneliness. The well had taken more than her light—it had taken her humanity.

In time, the stories began. Tales of a ghostly figure that roamed Bed-Stuy at night, watching over the borough with empty eyes. They called her the Shadow Princess, a guardian who had traded her soul for their salvation.

But the cost did not end there. Ginger's powers, though immense, came with limitations. She soon realized that her influence was fleeting. The joy she amplified faded like the morning dew, and the suffering she sought to erase returned tenfold. The whispers inside her laughed cruelly as she struggled to reconcile the futility of her efforts. Every act of kindness felt like pouring water into a sieve, her strength draining faster than the world could heal.

One night, as she wandered the streets, she encountered a young boy sitting alone on the stoop of a decrepit building. His eyes were hollow, his face streaked with tears. Ginger knelt before him, her shadowy form casting an eerie glow in the dim light of the streetlamp. "What's wrong, child?" she asked, her voice softer than she expected.

The boy looked up, startled by her presence, but something in her otherworldly gaze calmed him. "I'm scared," he whispered. "Mama said she'd be back, but she's not here. The lights went out, and it's so cold."

Ginger's heart ached. She extended her hand, and a warmth spread through her palm as she summoned a flicker of light. The boy's eyes widened as the light danced before him, illuminating the darkness. "Your mother will come back," she assured him. "Until then, you are not alone."

The boy smiled, a small, fragile thing that brought tears to Ginger's eyes. But as she withdrew her hand, she felt the whispers surge, mocking her for her sentimentality. The light she gave the boy began to fade almost immediately, and she watched helplessly as fear crept back into his eyes.

"Why does it go away?" the boy asked, his voice trembling.

Ginger had no answer. She rose to her feet, the weight of her failure pressing down on her shoulders. The whispers were relentless now, a cacophony of scorn that echoed in her mind. She turned away, her shadow stretching long and thin behind her as she disappeared into the night.

The days turned to weeks, and Ginger's resolve began to waver. The power she had traded her light for felt like a cruel joke, an illusion of control that left her more isolated than ever. The people of Bed-Stuy whispered about her in hushed tones, their fear of the Shadow Princess growing with each passing day. Parents warned their children to stay inside after dark, lest they catch a glimpse of the ghostly figure who roamed the streets.

Ginger's loneliness became unbearable. She longed for the warmth of human connection, the simple joy of a smile or a kind word. But every attempt to reach out was met with fear and rejection. The whispers inside her fed on her despair, growing louder and more insistent. They began to take on new forms, manifesting as shadowy figures that followed her wherever she went. They taunted her, their voices dripping with malice.

"You thought you could save them," one shadow hissed. "But you've only made things worse."

"Your sacrifice was in vain," another sneered. "You are nothing but a shadow, a relic of what once was."

Ginger tried to shut them out, but their words cut deep. She began to question her decision, wondering if she had been a fool to believe she could change the world. The well's promise had been a lie, a cruel trap that had ensnared her in an existence of endless torment.

She had wanted so desperately to save those around her, to lift them out of the despair that had consumed their lives and restore the light they'd lost. That desire, pure and burning, had driven her to the brink. But in her eagerness, her desperation, she had been blind to the trap laid before her. The promises of salvation, the whispered assurances that her sacrifice would bring peace, had been nothing more than illusions. She had been fooled—tricked into trading the very essence of who she was for a hollow, cold existence. The warmth that had once defined her, the compassion that had driven her actions, was gone. In its place was a void, a chill that seeped into every corner of her being.

And the worst part? She had saved no one. The people she had sought to protect were still suffering, their burdens as heavy as before. Her sacrifice had been in vain, a cruel twist of fate that left her not as a savior, but as another victim of the darkness she had tried to defeat. She had paid the ultimate price: her soul, her spirit, the very core of her humanity. All of it had been given up for a promise that had never been fulfilled.

She should have known. She should have realized that nothing in this world, not even salvation, came without a cost. But she had ignored the warnings, blinded by her own hope and determination. She was left to bear the weight of her decision—a cruel, eternal punishment for her naivety. The darkness had claimed her, twisting her into something unrecognizable, and it would never let her go.

Her once-vibrant soul, so full of light and love, was now cloaked in shadows. She could feel it, the cold tendrils of the darkness that had taken root inside her, suffocating the warmth that had once defined her. The very thing she had sought to fight had become a part of her, a constant reminder of her failure. And though she had given up everything, the world remained the same, unyielding and broken.

Her heart ached with the weight of her regret, a deep, unrelenting sorrow that threatened to consume her. She had been willing to give up everything for them, but in the end, she had only destroyed herself. And now, she stood alone in the shadows, her sacrifice unnoticed, her warmth forever lost to the cold embrace of the darkness.

***

One fateful night, as she wandered the streets, she found herself drawn to a familiar place. The forest. The Sundown Wild Forest, where her journey had begun. The trees loomed tall and menacing, their twisted branches casting eerie shadows in the moonlight. Ginger stepped onto the path, her footsteps silent as she made her way to the heart of the grove.

The blackened circle where the well had once stood was still there, a scar on the earth that pulsed with a faint, malevolent energy. Ginger knelt before it, her hands trembling as she traced the edges of the charred ground. "Why did you do this to me?" she whispered, her voice breaking. "Why did you make me believe I could make a difference?"

The whispers rose in a deafening chorus, their laughter echoing through the forest. "You chose this," they said. "You gave yourself to us willingly. Did you truly think you could bargain with the darkness?"

Ginger's tears fell freely, her shoulders shaking with the weight of her sorrow. She had lost everything—her light, her humanity, her place in the world. And for what? A power that could not truly heal, a gift that only brought pain.

But as she knelt there, something stirred within her. A spark of defiance, a flicker of the light she thought she had lost. She rose to her feet, her shadowy form towering over the blackened circle. "I may have given you my light," she said, her voice steady. "But you will not take my hope."

The whispers faltered, their laughter fading into silence. The shadows around her wavered, their forms growing less distinct. Ginger took a step forward, her resolve strengthening with each movement. "I will find a way to undo this," she said. "I will reclaim what you took from me. And I will not let you win."

For the first time since her transformation, the whispers were silent. The forest seemed to hold its breath as Ginger turned and walked away, her steps filled with purpose. The shadows followed her, but they no longer taunted her. Instead, they seemed to retreat, their presence growing fainter with each passing moment.

Ginger returned to Bed-Stuy, her heart heavy but her spirit unbroken. She knew the road ahead would be difficult, but she was determined to find a way to break the well's curse. She would face the darkness head-on, armed with the hope that had survived even the deepest despair.

And as she walked the streets of her neighborhood, the people began to notice a change. The ghostly figure they had feared was no longer a harbinger of doom but a beacon of quiet strength. The stories of the Shadow Princess began to shift, transforming from tales of terror to whispers of a guardian who fought tirelessly for her community.

Ginger's journey was far from over, but she had taken the first step toward redemption. And though the darkness still lingered, she knew she was not alone. The light within her, though dimmed, was not extinguished. It burned on, a testament to the resilience of the human spirit and the enduring power of hope.

Tessa Lee-Thomas

Tessa Lee-Thomas is a Brooklyn-based writer, nursing student, and doula with a passion for storytelling that explores the intersections of fear, resilience, and womanhood. Inspired by the complexities of Black identity, she crafts chilling narratives that center Black women's experiences in the horror genre.

Afterword
J. V. Sadler

Take a breath. *Whew*! You are safe now.

In this Afterword, I will say a little bit about the journey to *Mama Said*, then say a few words about my thoughts on each story, including my own. I also want to end with an address to the still-blossoming Black women writers who are reading this—I see you!

The Road to *Mama Said*

The journey to *Mama Said* looks like a "U." I started the project with so much vigor, motivation, and inspiration. After having formed the planning team, so much good was happening, it was as if we could see the anthology in our hands before we had even brainstormed one idea. We had meeting after meeting. Had a solid plan. Then . . . the first Kickstarter fundraiser failed. Kickstarter, for those who may not know, is a popular crowdsourcing site where creators open fundraisers for their projects. In exchange for financial support, those financial backers would get different perks. Our perks included free ebook and paperback copies of the anthology, a special hardcover edition, inclusion in the Thank You pages, and a bookmark. I would be remiss to say that the Kickstarter failure didn't *kick* the wind out of my sails. I can't speak for the others on the planning team, but I know that I was ready to give up.

After that experience, I would then face an onslaught of busyness in my life. I earned my Master's degree (thanks for your applause!), but would also face some personal difficulties, such as trying to tame and wrangle my Bipolar II condition. I went from being on top of the world to being at the bottom of the barrel. *Mama Said* had to take a backseat in my life. At some point, so many months had passed that I was afraid the selected authors would back out of the project. I had to come to terms with the possibility that I'd let everyone down. The best thing I could do was be transparent, be honest, and take responsibility for any outcome.

This is where the last half of the "U" comes in. I am thankful to the planning team and the selected authors for their patience, understanding, and grace towards this project. Their words of encouragement and the planning team's insistence on trying again after we didn't meet our first fundraising goal reignited my passion for the project. It warmed my soul to see that people believed in *Mama Said.*

The rest, as they say, is history.

Ten Stories

I've spoken about the anthology's unifying themes and messages as a whole. Getting a closer look at each story, helps understand where each puzzle piece fits in the collective picture that is *Mama Said.* Note, I won't spoil any of the story surprises in the odd case that someone is scanning through the Afterword before reading all of the anthology.

We start the anthology with a BANG with **"To Double Dutch the Devil" by E.A. Noble.** Situated in Mississippi, a group of Black girls has an ambitious dream: a dream that one girl would do anything to win. I highly relate to this big dreaming group, as I think many would. When big dreams overshadow the greatness happening in the present reality, sometimes we forget the community of love we're surrounded by, bypass those who support us, and ignore the entire creative journey towards whatever it is that we love. Fortunately, Noble ends on a great note that is clever and uplifting.

"The Closet Window" by Lori Titus plays on every childhood fear: the creepy closet. Again, it's something that most people can relate to in their childhoods, whether turning off the light then bolting to the bed to outrun the imaginary monster or checking underneath the bed then refusing to let a limb hang off the edge so that the monster starves for the night. My question is, was it all in the child's vivid imagination what she saw (I think I've jumped a few times seeing shadows out of the corners of my eyes)? Or, was it terrifyingly real? I think the story's ending will help clarify.

"Deadly Visions" by Vivienne Neal is a short piece that brings some big drama. I see a love triangle, I bring my popcorn. The story seems to be split into two: the very reasonable, normal introduction and the moment when things take a turn for the worse . . . and it just gets progressively worse from there. As a reader, I felt conflicted about which person(s) to feel sorry for. Maybe it's no one in this story who is redeemable.

"The Mystery of Shepherd's Pie" by C.Y. Marshall is a story that may feel familiar to those who are fans of detective shows or unsolved mystery stories. The readers are dropped into this town with already so much baggage. Really, I feel for this town and the crimes that have ensued years in the making. But what starts as a possible serial killer or kidnapping situation turns much more sinister and supernatural. Interesting how trauma can sometimes find itself back to us. What would we do if our most difficult childhood memories came back to find us as adults? What if we realize they never left us to begin with? I was eating while reading this story. Major mistake.

"Clean, Miranda, Clean" by N.M. Chaney is the anthology's middle story. It's the turning point from the first half

into the second half. We follow Miranda when she . . . well .
. . cleans. There is much history in this story that the author
chooses not to fully reveal. Instead, the author is forced to
stay in this bloody moment, confused and scared of what will
happen next. We often clean to music, right? Towards the
end of the story, there are a few musical elements—a playlist
of sorts. Try listening to your own playlist and imagine Miranda cleaning.

"The Hollow Crown" by Anniee Bee marks the second
half of the anthology. It's another short and sweet story that
leans heavily into the fantastical storytelling elements. The
story is split into parts or mini-flash pieces that tell the story
of a cursed kingdom. The piece uses stylized language to
capture the aesthetic of our favorite fantasy tales. By the end
of the story, I contemplate how much we can escape our fates
(if fate and destiny exist). No matter how much we try to
change things, sometimes we are meant for something. Bee
twists this concept—what if that something we are meant
for is evil?

"The Girl Without a Face" by J.V. Sadler (me!) tells the story of finding oneself, identity, and creating oneself. But sometimes that process of renaming oneself can be painful and bloody. In the story, I transport the reader to an unnamed archaic, simpler time. The girl utilizes the help of a new friend to escape the town's bullying. Through the pain, she finds power. By the end of the story, the girl finally finds who she is. Oh! Just as a heads up, when you read the title, take it literally.

"Whispers in the Wood" by Ginny Davis is a shorter piece that uses dark fantasy as a vehicle for environmental justice. In the first paragraph, we are introduced to a character, a tree nymph, who brings a sense of whimsy and wonder. Even when the character faces a dire situation, I couldn't help but feel giddy over a simple yet so comfortable story. I was thrown back to my first time watching *The NeverEnding Story* or even the Barbie *Mariposa* series. It is the hero's journey summed up in two pages. Also, it always feels good seeing a story about standing up to, essentially, deforesters.

"RAVEN" by Miracle Austin is filled with so much emotion and drama and life lessons and rage and revenge and . . . Well, in this story, you'll be rooting for the girls. The story's unexpected ending has me reflecting on the power that each of us, no matter how timid, has within. This story seems to be a call for, yes, self-love but also being bold with that self-love. In times of chaos, when we remember who we are, we can make magic (sometimes literally)! If this story has you gritting your teeth in anger, don't worry. You will get your eventual satisfaction.

We end the anthology with **"The Whispering Well" by Tessa Lee-Thomas**. This story is timely for today's political sphere. It expresses all the fears and obstacles that those who are trying to make a difference in their communities may face. The supernatural, dark, fantastical elements are all too real. For anyone striving for social change, I believe this story might hit too close to home. Ginger, the main character, is many of us. The story concludes with much-needed hope. In fact, its last word is "hope." We start the anthology in Mississippi and end in Bed-Stuy—a worthy journey for *Mama Said*!

An Address to the still-blossoming Black woman writer

Dear still-blossoming Black woman writer,

I think it's about time, and you know what that means. Have you seen your creative lineage? The well of greatness that Black writers pull from? In the moments when your pen refuses to ink the page, when the keyboard refuses to type, when your voice recordings become strange and inaudible—know that you have never been alone. You are not the first to look at their story and cringe at the undeveloped draft. You won't be the last to consider giving up on their creativity. Please, write one more word. When you've written one more word, you have successfully resisted the forces that would want to siphon your creative superpower in the name of greed, consumption, and exploitation.

It's okay to pause. Sometimes a break may last a day. Sometimes it may last years. But know that your creativity will always be here, waiting for you. When you finally open up that dusty notebook or search for that old folder on your computer, your writing will welcome you with a smile. Thank you for your art.

Not every story will be The One. Not every contest will be won. Not every writer will become a household name. What is unequivocally true, though art sustains all of time. Art heals. Art transgresses. Art challenges us to become our full selves. Art appreciates you.

To the Black woman writer who may be doubting herself, who may be faltering, or who may be tired of fighting and fighting, I have to say that I am so proud of you. Rest if you must; Transform if you will. Please find a soft place for your art, and if that place does not exist, please create it. The Black girls who are writing after us will thank you for it. And if you haven't been told lately, I love you.

Sincerely,

J.V. Sadler